A PUZZLING POOCH AND PUMPKIN PUFFS

ALSO BY ALEKSA BAXTER

MAGGIE MAY AND MISS FANCYPANTS MYSTERIES

A DEAD MAN AND DOGGIE DELIGHTS

A CRAZY CAT LADY AND CANINE CRUNCHIES

A BURIED BODY AND BARKERY BITES

A MISSING MOM AND MUTT MUNCHIES

A SABOTAGED CELEBRATION AND SALMON SNAPS

A POISONED PAST AND PUPPERMINTS

🐾🐾🐾

A FOULED-UP FOURTH

A SALACIOUS SCANDAL AND STEAK SIZZLERS

A PUZZLING POOCH AND PUMPKIN PUFFS

NOSY NEWFIE HOLIDAY SHORTS

HALLOWEEN AT THE BAKER VALLEY BARKERY & CAFE

A HOUSEBOUND HOLIDAY

A PUZZLING POOCH

AND PUMPKIN PUFFS

A MAGGIE MAY AND MISS FANCYPANTS MYSTERY

ALEKSA BAXTER

CHAPTER 1

Do you want to know the worst words in the English language? Bed rest. Bad enough that I was the size of a small house and had all sorts of things going on with my body that I had never wanted to experience thanks to the two bumps of joy I was incubating inside me.

But now…

Now my doctor, Dr. Dillon—an attractive middle-aged woman who was way too pleasant even when delivering bad news—had just told me that I had to go on bed rest.

I stared into her sympathetic eyes and wanted to do violence.

Instead I took three, deep, calming breaths, and reminded myself it wasn't her fault. Really. It wasn't. Truly. Not her fault. Not anyone's. Just…biology. Sometimes these things happen, especially when you're pregnant with twins.

Finally, when I thought I had calmed down enough not to scream, I asked, "For how long?"

"Until the babies come."

No. Not possible.

"That could be another two months."

"Hopefully." She smiled and it took every ounce of reserve I had not to tell her to stop being so frickin' calm and cheerful already. She squeezed my hand. "Every single day we can get is a day closer to those babies being just fine when they're born."

Right. It was all about the babies now. I was just an incubator trying to get them across the finish line.

Nobody talks about that part of having kids. The worry that they won't turn out all healthy and perfect. That there might be weeks or months at the hospital after the birth.

At least not much. It's like this collective forgetfulness that constantly happens.

I had one friend who had a kid with a collapsed lung in utero. The doctors had to go in there with some sort of needle and inflate it while she was still pregnant. But did anyone mention it after the procedure? Noooo. All good. Just a minor collapsed lung. No biggie. Carry on.

Gah!

I stared at the monitor with my two little girls on it and sighed. "Fine. Bed rest. Do I get to pee on my own at least or is there something fun I get to use for that?"

Matt, my tall, dark, and gorgeous husband who I wanted to strangle for being half of what got me into this situation, kissed my forehead. "It's okay, Maggie. Two more months and then they'll be here. You can do this."

Easy for him to say. He wasn't the one going to be stuck in bed for the next two months and then have to get them out on top of that. He just had to show up and cut the umbilical cord and show the babies around to everyone.

Must be nice.

(I know, I know. I wasn't being fair to him. He had to stand by, mostly powerless, for nine months while I grew two little lives inside me. Honestly, that lack of control would've upset me more than everything I'd already been through and was about to go through. But still. I had to have some sort of target for all of my anxiety and he was right there.)

The doctor smiled and nodded her head slightly. "You can pee on your own. Just try, as much as possible, to rest and stay calm. Every moment you can do that is better for the babies."

I glanced at my very, very large stomach. "You two hear that? I'm doing this for you. So when you're fifteen and try to sneak out of the house and I'm too darned tired to stop you because I'm *old*, you think about your poor mother and what she sacrificed to get you here. And then you turn yourselves around and go back to bed. I couldn't even do all-nighters in college, I'm definitely not doing them for two little hellions who've snuck out of the house for some stupid boy or party."

Matt chuckled. "Don't worry. I think that falls under dad duty. I'll be sitting on the porch waiting for them."

"Good. Because I will need every minute of beauty sleep I can get by that point." I sighed and glanced back to the doctor. "I assume this means I can't walk my dog anymore?"

"Absolutely not. No dog walking."

That was not going to go over well. Fancy, my almost five-year-old Newfoundland, loved her walks. And she was quite vocal about when she needed one.

Matt rubbed my shoulder. "I'll walk her. Or your grandpa can."

I laughed. "My grandpa? I can just imagine that conversation right now. *What do you mean she needs a walk? She has a yard already, why would she need a walk on top of that? You spoil her.*"

"He'll do it for you, though. You know he will. And you know he'll probably enjoy it. He tries to hide it, but he has a soft spot for Fancy."

"Yeah, you're probably right. But what about the resort? We're finally gearing up for opening. I was going to do things."

"Leave that to Jamie. And Greta. And Mason. And me if it comes to it. You're not alone in this Maggie."

Thankfully. I'd at one brief point in time before I met Matt thought about having a kid on my own. I was my parents' only child and it was all down to me to pass along their genes so I felt this sort of weird guilt that I hadn't yet.

But…doing it alone?

Hahaha. Oh hell no.

I mean, yes, of course, it was amazing and wonderful to bring beautiful children into the world and having a child is one of the best things most people have ever done in their lives. And women make it work on their own all the time. Yadda, yadda, yadda.

Let's not pretend any of it is easy.

Ask a mom of a two-year-old if you should have a kid on your own and she will laugh hysterically while trying not to fall asleep mid-conversation.

I was so glad to have Matt and everyone else around to help. And even then…bed rest. And who knew what would come after that. No one could help with that part. It was all me.

Yes, yes, I know. Negative Nelly. But better to think the worst and get the best than think the best and get the worst. That's my motto at least.

I prefer to be pleasantly surprised when life doesn't turn out to be a dumpster fire. And when it does, like when your doctor puts you on bed rest for two months, well, you figure out the best path forward and roll with it because you were never expecting it to be smooth sailing anyway.

Might not make me a good party guest or person to have a conversation with, but at least I can roll with the punches when they inevitably come.

CHAPTER 2

As we took our papers and Matt helped me navigate the waiting room like some sort of tanker ship at risk of blocking half of the world's shipping supply, he said, "Maybe we should move down to Denver until the baby's born. Stay somewhere near a hospital. It's probably safe enough to do so now."

He had a point. I mean, living in small-town Colorado is great. Clean air, beautiful mountains, quiet. But when there's a medical issue…That helicopter flight to Denver could be the difference between making it and not.

Assuming the flight could even go, because April in Colorado is not always bright and sunny. We've had snows as late as June, although May is much more likely to be the last month of snow.

Either way, chances were, whenever the babies arrived it would still be snow season, which meant regardless of my own preferences I'd probably be giving birth at the local hospital unless we stationed ourselves down in Denver.

And I might not even make it to the local hospital. It was a solid twenty minutes from Creek in good weather.

A Puzzling Pooch and Pumpkin Puffs

Did I really want to be at home, realize I needed to get to the hospital NOW, and not be able to get there? When something as delicate and precious as my two babies was at risk?

I shuddered as Matt helped me down the two steps on the front porch. (The doctor's office had at one point been a small house that was then converted over to medical offices. It still had the white picket fence, which was just weird in my book. I like my doctor's offices sterile and unfriendly, not a cheery bright yellow. But it was what it was.)

I sighed.

The stress of it all was overwhelming. I'd thought taking care of a dog was hard. Being pregnant was a whole new level of anxiety involving weird bodily changes and hormone surges. But it was too late to turn back now.

(Not that I would want to. Babies. Yay.)

"What about your job?" I asked. "You can't just not go for two months."

"I'll take the time off."

"Will they let you?" I couldn't imagine a small-town police force had paternity leave. Not like we lived in Sweden.

"You and these babies are more important to me than anything, Maggie."

He helped me into the back of the minivan we'd bought the week before. My van without any backseats and his truck weren't exactly ideal vehicles for transporting kiddos around after all. (Or hugely-pregnant women for that matter.)

It was awkward sitting in the back like some sort of celebrity with a chauffeur, but I'd hit the point where a normal front passenger seat could not accommodate my very large belly. Not to mention all the lovely statistics Matt had shared with me about people in front passenger seats and car wrecks. Something I could have gone my whole life without knowing, thank you very much.

As he drove us back towards home, I picked up the conversation once more. "I know you want to take care of us, but I don't want you to lose your job over it. Maybe my grandpa and Lesley could come down to Denver with me. Or…well, not Jamie. She's hip-deep in the resort preparations. And she has Max to worry about. Same with Greta. At least as far as the resort is concerned. Plus, being away for two months…Ugh. Also, are we really sure it's safe now? I mean, things certainly seem safer…"

"If you go to Denver, I go with you."

"But work. You can't just take off like that and expect to come back. You know that."

He drummed his fingers on the steering wheel. "I've been meaning to talk to you about that, actually."

I tensed. "Talk to me about what?"

He stared straight ahead, not glancing in my direction as he turned onto the two-lane highway towards home.

Uh-oh. This was going to be bad.

He didn't say anything as we accelerated down the road, the snow-covered mountains rising up on either side of us, covered in evergreens, the sky a pure, soft blue with no sign of a storm in sight.

Finally, I couldn't stand the silence anymore. "Matt, I am a hormonal pregnant woman who has just been told she's going to have to lie in weird positions for the next two months so she doesn't accidentally drop her babies out before they're due. It would be a good idea to get to the point and not spike my blood pressure any more than it already is."

"I'm thinking of quitting my job." The words tumbled out so fast I barely understood what he'd said.

"What? Why? I thought you liked it? I mean, I know it was hard at first having to arrest people you grew up with, but I thought you'd moved past that. I thought you were angling for a promotion even."

He nodded. "I did. And I was." His fingers clenched the steering wheel until his knuckles turned white.

"But then I got pregnant."

He shrugged one shoulder. If he hadn't been driving a motor vehicle at sixty miles an hour down a two-lane highway and I wasn't the size of a large walrus, I would've grabbed his chin and forced him to look my way.

"Matt, talk to me. Do you want to quit or do you think you have to?"

He sighed and finally glanced my way in the rearview mirror. "A little of both."

"Explain."

He let a deep breath out before he answered. "I talked to the Chief about that promotion. I couldn't be based out of Creek, which means a longer commute unless we move."

"Which we've discussed. Moving would put us closer to the resort, too, so it makes some sense to do it."

"But it puts us farther away from your grandpa and Lesley. The Chief also said if I wanted more responsibility then I'd have to be prepared to give more at work. Longer hours, filling in unexpectedly when someone's sick or a situation requires extra staff. As a supervisor I'd be that go-to person. Lots of late-night call outs. Leaving you home alone with two babies."

I won't lie. The thought of being alone in the middle of the night with two screaming babies scared the you-know-what out of me.

But Matt was my husband and life is never perfect. You always have to make some compromise or another. Always.

"We can make it work, Matt. If that's what you want. The promotion, all of it. We'll find a way. If we stay in Creek my grandpa is right there. He can always come over and help if I need it."

"He's not young, Maggie."

"No, but I don't think he's leaving us anytime soon either. Knock wood. He's gotten his shots now and he's as protected as he can be at this point. Plus, you know he's an ornery bugger who'll probably be here until he's a hundred. We can make it work, Matt, if that's what you want."

He clenched his jaw. "My dad wasn't really there for us, you know. He provided, we always had a roof over our head, but he wasn't there. I don't want to do that to my kids. I want to see their first steps and hear their first words."

"Oh, Matt." I would've squeezed his shoulder, but I couldn't move far enough to reach him. "Okay. I get it. If you want to quit, we'll figure it out."

Of course, I was panicking inside. I was about to bring two little lives into the world and we were going to need to feed them, which meant income. You can't exactly live outside in the Colorado mountains even if I were so inclined.

So, you know, we needed a plan. I just hoped he had one. Because I was supposed to not be stressing. "Do you have any idea what you want to do instead?" I asked, hopefully.

I winced as the words left my mouth, because it was not the most diplomatic thing to ask, but I had to ask or else my mind was going to spiral out of control with doomsday scenarios of my supporting two babies and a husband on the income from a pet resort that could very well fail.

He was back to not looking at me. "I thought maybe the resort could use a head of security. Mason mentioned something about it the last time I saw him."

I opened my mouth and closed it again. If Matt went to work for the resort, too, and it failed…Then we'd have nothing.

I drummed my fingers on the armrest.

Nothing.

But I couldn't say that. Matt clearly didn't need to hear that right then.

Marriage is so darned hard. Being supportive when you are a practical person is not always easy, especially when your life is not yet settled into a steady track.

"Do you want to call him about it?" I asked. "Or I can."

Secretly I was screaming for him to please call now so I knew that he'd have a job for at least the first three months of the babies' lives.

"I'll do it. And if that doesn't work out, I'll figure something else out. Don't worry." He flashed me a quick grin over his shoulder. "We won't starve, Maggie, I promise. We might not be eating steaks off of china plates, but as long as you're okay with the occasional hot dog off of a paper plate, I'll always provide for you."

I forced a smile when he glanced back at me even though I was silently cataloging everything I owned and how much it could be sold for and how long our savings would last on one income and what we could do if the resort failed and how likely it was I could get some consulting work if I needed it.

But all I said was, "I know you will. I trust you."

Because *that* is love. Smiling at your husband when all he can provide is hot dogs on paper plates even if you'd prefer steaks on china. Because you can't imagine anyone else you'd rather spend your life with and all you want is to see him happy.

And, really. In the grand scheme of things what are steaks and china next to a life partner you wouldn't want to live without? Right?

Right.

CHAPTER 3

Within days Matt had it all sorted. It was kind of amazing really.

We decided not to go down to Denver. That was a little too far from our support system and Matt had agreed to keep working as a cop until the babies were born so they could find a replacement for him. As you can imagine, cop wasn't the most in-demand job in early 2021.

By staying in the Baker Valley we could also arrange for a rotating set of people to drop in and check on me on a regular basis when he had to work. And there would actually be people I could call in an emergency other than him.

We did move into one of the cabins at the resort that had already been completed, though. Partially to be closer to the hospital, partially to let me do some work and meet with at least Greta and Jamie when needed.

Also, because I was a little freaked out about living in a home with stairs being as pregnant as I was. I'd had a pregnant friend I'd made online fall down the stairs the week before. She was fine—just a quick trip to the ER and some pain for a few days—but that was it for me.

Stairs and I have never been friends to begin with. Add in a huge belly that didn't let me see my feet and there was no way I was going near them again until after I'd given birth. Add bed rest into the picture on top of all of that and I was just done with that place.

The cabin was located about a mile from the main resort buildings and nestled amongst the trees around a small pond along with about a dozen other cabins. Each one was fully-furnished with a good-sized bedroom, bathroom with both a tub and a shower, a small combined dining and living room area, and a full kitchen.

It actually reminded me a bit of some of the cabins I'd stayed at when backpacking through New Zealand, with the exception of the kitchen and bathroom. Most of the ones in New Zealand had a communal kitchen and bathroom area, but we'd decided that wouldn't work as well with the high-end resort feel we were going for.

(I say we, but I mean the people who were actually high-end in our little venture, namely, Mason, Greta, and Jamie. Me, I was a little bit closer to being trailer park trash than a denizen of a high-end luxury accommodation.)

Because our property was a pet resort the cabin also had a back porch and small fenced-in yard that Fancy could reach via a doggie door. I'd insisted that the doggie doors be large enough for a dog Fancy's size even though everyone had argued with me that with bears and mountain lions and what-not in the area that it maybe wasn't the best idea.

Ultimately, I'd pulled pregnant hormonal woman privilege and gotten my way, but we'd compromised and only three of the cabins had the extra-large doggie doors. Also, visitors had to sign a waiver that they understood the risk of actually using the doors.

(Mason being a lawyer there were lots of waivers for guests to sign. I swear, he'd probably included a waiver for staying at high-altitudes in there, just in case. I miss the days when people were expected to know the risks they were taking rather than go through life mindlessly until something bad happened to them and then find an appropriate party to sue for not telling them that life ultimately ends in death, and that that death can arrive in about a million different ways on any given day. But America being America I was also glad to have someone like Mason on the case. Better to cover too much than too little when it comes to potential lawsuits.)

Even though I was close enough for meetings, we limited my visitors to my grandpa, Matt, Jamie, Greta, and Mason, all wearing masks. That's because we'd been forced to remove the barriers to the valley the week before and none of us were sure what that would mean for case counts.

As soon as the barriers came down the valley was immediately flooded with the "this was never a big deal, you joy killers just wanted to keep us from our lives" crowd, so those of us who did think it was a big deal were being forced to be careful.

My grandpa and Lesley were fully vaccinated and the rest of us had managed one shot so far, but the last thing I wanted when I was two months from delivering twins was to get a respiratory illness that was best treated by putting patients on their bellies. I was pretty sure that wasn't going to work all that well in my case.

So, yeah, my life was a lot of "fun" between bed rest, limited visitors, and masking. Good times.

Of course, me being me, I'd done my own research about bed rest and come to a slightly different conclusion than the doctor.

After careful review of numerous sources, I had decided to take into account the spirit of the recommendation from my doctor— to take it easy, don't stress out, and don't take undue risks with my body— without actually spending twenty-four hours a day in bed—which would have spiked my anxiety levels so high I would've probably gone into labor within a week.

In my defense, it turned out not every doctor agreed that bed rest actually did anything useful for prolonging a pregnancy. In fact, some thought it made things worse because the forced inactivity led to blood clots.

I wanted to listen to my doctor, I did, but sometimes with medicine you have to find your own balance, you know? And sometimes doctors are so busy being doctors and trying to squeeze in personal lives on the margins that they don't have time to keep up with all of the latest research.

(Although, as the world had so recently shown, not everyone is qualified to make their own medical decisions. Because sometimes when people take medical decisions into their own hands they end up taking horse dewormer for no good reason. Seriously, people. Learn how to figure out when you're being scammed.)

Anyway.

I was staying at the cabin full-time and no walks for Fancy to be safe, but I'd decided I could at least make myself meals and sit at the dining room table or on the couch if I wanted.

A Puzzling Pooch and Pumpkin Puffs

I actually didn't mind being isolated at the cabin. It had the nice side benefit of keeping me away from weird-ass strangers who wanted to touch me all the time. And, yes, I did just cuss, but I mean, what is it about a pregnant woman that people suddenly think they have the right to *touch* her?

"Oh, look. You're pregnant." Hand on stomach.

Do not do that to me. Do not touch me. I am a person who hurts first and asks questions later.

Which is why it was probably a very good thing I was restricted to the cabin for the rest of my pregnancy, since I was pretty sure Matt would not want to arrest his very pregnant wife for slugging some old lady in the grocery store.

(You should've seen the death stare I gave some woman who told me I wasn't allowed caffeine when she saw me drinking a Coke. Lady, mind your own. I talked to my doctor about it, thank you very much.)

Anyway. Being away from the stomach-touchers and this-is-how-you-should-do-pregnancy-opiners was very soothing in and of itself. Brought my blood pressure right down.

But poor Fancy was completely lost.

She's a champ, but the last two years had been a lot of change and stress. The cabin was her fourth home in that time and then there I was suddenly growing this huge belly and acting weird. It was a lot.

She wouldn't let me out of her sight. It was all I could do to get her to go outside and do her business. The rest of the time she spent within about three feet of me.

Which I appreciated, I did. I liked the company. Especially with Matt doing so many double shifts and being gone most nights. (He was doing the double shifts partially from guilt over quitting his job and partially in an attempt to build up a little extra money before the babies came, since we didn't know what challenges that might bring.)

So I liked the company, I did. It's just that Fancy's really big. And sometimes she would position herself so that I had to try to maneuver around her and, well, I was big, too, and the combination did not work out well. I almost tripped on her at least a dozen times the first two weeks we were there.

Anyway.

That's all a long explanation of how I found myself awake in the dark at midnight in an isolated cabin listening to the sound of the over-sized doggie door thwack back and forth as something or someone pushed through it.

CHAPTER 4

At first I thought the noise I'd heard was Fancy going outside in the middle of the night—she'd definitely done that at the old house—but no. Fancy was snoring away on the floor right next to me.

Soooo, not Fancy.

Which meant…

A bear?

A mountain lion?

A scary serial killer stalking hugely pregnant women?

Probably not that last one. Of course, that still left the bear or mountain lion options. I winced, thinking about how my grandpa was going to tell me he'd told me so, because he'd warned me it wasn't a good idea to have a doggie door in the mountains and now here he was, proved right.

Fancy, through some miracle, was still snoring as I heard nails scramble on the kitchen tile. I froze, wondering what to do next.

I didn't want to wake Fancy. If it was a bear or a mountain lion she wouldn't have a chance against it. I mean I've heard of Newfies that defended their owners against wild animals like that, but Fancy was not going to be one of them. She's a marshmallow.

I did have a steak knife somewhere on the dresser, but I wasn't sure what good it would do me.

(Yes, I'm weird, thank you very much. But I'd spent most of my life as a single woman living alone. And it's comforting to have a random sharp object you can scramble for in the dark should the worst happen. Not that I'd be able to use it effectively if it ever came to that, but it did at least let me sleep better at night.)

Well. I figured a knife in hand was better than nothing, so I patted around trying to find it hoping that Matt hadn't put it away—he was not a fan of random sharp objects in the bedroom, don't know why.

I couldn't see anything and didn't want to turn on a light, so it was not easy to find the knife. Also, my gaze was fixed on that dark doorway just waiting for whatever it was to make its appearance.

A floorboard creaked in the living room and Fancy snorted and sat up.

Crap.

She jumped to her feet and ran out of the room, barking, before I could stop her. I heard nails on the kitchen tiles and then the doggie door flapped. Once. Twice.

Great. Now Fancy was outside with whatever it was.

At least that meant I could turn on the bedside lamp without alerting the creature to my presence. I did so and carefully levered myself to my feet, cussing the whole time about how awkward it is to move when you have a gigantic mass sticking out from the middle of your body that no amount of widening pelvis can account for.

Once I was sure I wouldn't fall back onto the bed, I grabbed the knife in one hand and my cellphone in the other, and took a step towards the doorway.

The doggie door flapped again, once.

"Fancy?" I called as I hit the speed dial option for Matt.

She didn't come into the room, but the doggie door flapped again. Were both of them inside now? Or had the one that had come back, gone back outside?

"Fancy?" I asked more hesitantly, taking another step towards the doorway.

"Maggie?" Matt answered the phone, sounding breathless. "Everything okay?"

"I don't know."

"Are you in labor? Do I need to get home?"

"No...Not in labor..." I finally made it to the doorway but everything was dark. I really had to pee, too. That was not helping.

"Maggie. What is it then? I'm...in the midst of something here."

"Fancy?" I called again as I heard movement from the living room.

I stopped next to the door. Should I close it? That would lock Fancy outside the bedroom with whatever it was and I didn't want to do that. But I also didn't want to meet a deer or bear or mountain lion or...whatever. Me and my little steak knife weren't exactly going to do anything useful against it.

"Maggie," Matt snapped. "What is going on?"

I continued to peer into the darkness. "Something came in the doggie door. Fancy went after it. And now I think they're both in the living room. Either that or they're both outside. I don't know what it was. I'm gonna go see."

I took another step forward.

"No. Don't. Stay in the bedroom, Maggie. I'll be there in five minutes."

"It's fine. You're busy. Fancy isn't crying out or anything. I'm sure it's just a…I don't know. But I'm sure it's fine. Go back to work."

"Stay in your room, Maggie. I'll be right there." He hung up.

I stood there, desperately needing to pee, wondering where Fancy was and what was out there with her, and wondering exactly how long Matt was really going to take to arrive. Because I was pretty sure he was not five minutes away.

Probably more like ten.

And I couldn't wait that long. I needed to pee. And I was not going to just casually pee when I didn't know what was in my home.

Steeling myself against what I might find, I tightened my grip on the knife, groped around on the wall until I found the switch, and flipped on the light.

CHAPTER 5

I didn't realize I'd been holding my breath until I choked on it.

I'd been so ready for a bear, or a moose, or a mountain lion. What I had not expected was a little fluff ball of a dog. It was pure mutt. All multi-colored black, brown, and white, with floppy ears.

And probably not exactly small to anyone else, but Fancy is a hundred and thirty-five pounds and this little guy was half her size.

He saw me and his whole body started vibrating with excitement, but he didn't move because Fancy was there between us.

"It's okay, Fancy." I stepped closer and rested my hand on her back. "You're fine. Let him be. Hi there, fella." He wiggled his whole body even more as I talked to him.

But now that the threat was past, I really, really needed to pee. "Be right back," I told them.

I know, I should've blocked them in different parts of the cabin or something. But right then all I could think about was the intense pressure on my bladder. Sorry. TMI.

I ran into the bathroom. I figured they'd stay where they were until I came back. At least Fancy would. And I was right, she was still there when I emerged a couple minutes later.

But our visitor was gone.

"Where'd he go, Fancy?" I asked. She looked at me with those intelligent amber eyes of hers, but didn't move. "Where's the dog?"

She ran around the living room, sniffing, but then came back to me.

"You understand that didn't help, right? I could've done a lap around the living room myself, you know."

I winced. I'd been trying to only be loving and affirmative with Fancy since I'd found out I was pregnant. I figured it was good practice for when the babies came and they could actually understand what I said and hold it against me when they were older.

Seriously. It's not like every single off-hand comment has to be taken literally. Come on. But with kids...Yeah.

As you can see, I wasn't doing well with my attempts to limit my sarcastic nature which is why I figured I'd just have to start putting a dollar away towards the kids' therapy fund every time I said something less than perfect.

I figured with interest and compounding it would hopefully be enough to get them started with therapy at least.

Plus, the good thing about those sorts of comments is they would probably drive my kids to be relentless overachievers, so they'd have some funds of their own to work from which I could indirectly claim credit for, thereby creating yet another therapy spiral where they questioned their entire existence and whether their personal success was in fact a direct result of their overly-sarcastic mother and her comments.

I would've probably stood there having an existential crisis for the rest of the night, but Matt arrived. He dashed through the door looking all adorably frazzled. "I'm here."

"I see that."

"Are you okay?" He grabbed my arms and looked me over.

"I'm fine. Go back to work. You were in the middle of something when I called. I'm sorry to pull you away for nothing."

"Just some kids spray-painting a few stop signs. I almost had one of them, but then the phone rang."

"And you stopped to answer it?" I teared up at the thought. Pregnancy hormones, I tell ya. "You didn't need to do that for me."

"You could've been in labor."

"Oh, yeah. True…Okay, fine. Sorry. Always answer when I call."

"I do." He kissed me on the forehead. "So where's the intruder?"

"Gone. It was a dog. A very cute dog. Some sort of mutt. But it left when I went to the bathroom."

Matt glanced at the doggie door. "We did tell you…"

"Yeah, yeah. Mountain lion. Bear. Blah, blah. But Fancy likes to be able to go in and out. And it's a lot easier than me having to get up to let her out each time." I patted my belly. He'd watched the conniptions I went through each time I had to stand up. He knew.

But…

We both stared at the doggie door.

I really didn't want a bear to come inside. But I also didn't want to deal with a Fancy who was blocked in. She's very high-pitched when she wants to be. And relentless. She'll make a sad little cry in the back of her throat every ten seconds until she gets her way.

Matt slid the cover in to block the doggie door. "Just for tonight."

"But what about the stray? Now it can't come back."

"Did it look like a stray? Maybe it just ran away from home and has now run back."

I chewed on my lip, thinking about it. "I don't know. I didn't get a very good look. It definitely wasn't starving, but it didn't look like it just came from someone's house either."

He squeezed my arms. "It'll be fine. Dogs are good at finding their way home. And this way you aren't waking up to a dog fight in the yard in the middle of the night."

I looked at Fancy who had sprawled by the front door. Yeah, dog fight. Right. Only if it could be done while lying down in a comfortable position.

(Although, Fancy has had her moments. She has a one-handed takedown I've seen her use on other dogs before, but then she doesn't really know what to do from there other than stand above them and growl the dog-equivalent of "leave me alone you annoying little dog". I don't know what she'd do if a dog actually tried to attack her…Then again, I didn't want to find out either.)

I glanced at the closed doggie door. That dog had looked harmless. And it was cold out. But…

One of the twins decided to kick me in the kidneys. Ow.

A Puzzling Pooch and Pumpkin Puffs

I was worried about that dog, but not as much as I wanted to go back to bed. "Okay. Yeah, fine. Thank you for running home to protect me." I kissed him on the cheek. "Love you."

"Love you, too."

Fancy followed me into the bedroom and curled up at the end of the bed while Matt let himself out the front door.

As I listened to the sound of his police vehicle driving away and tried to find a comfortable position around my absurdly-shaped but oh-so-necessary pillow, I wondered who the dog belonged to and if Matt was right that it would find its way back home.

I sure hoped so. But before I could worry about it too much I fell back asleep.

CHAPTER 6

The next morning I couldn't stop thinking about that poor dog. What if he hadn't found his way home? What if he'd spent the night shivering under a bush somewhere because he hadn't been able to get back inside the cabin?

I decided I could at least look around the yard and see if there was any sign of him. That shouldn't be too risky for me and the babies. It was just the yard. And it was small.

It had snowed a bit overnight so I had to bundle up. Since I couldn't manage boots I had gone down the dreaded Crocs path. I'd somehow avoided that particular awful fashion trend the first time around, but with my feet so swollen and not being able to put on shoes that tied or slipped over my heel, they were a blessing.

They even had lined ones. I had a pair of blue, green, and purple ones that had a black lining that didn't look too old-lady. (Although they were definitely, "I've given up on being fashionable and just want to be comfortable", which I had decided was my new fashion aesthetic.)

A Puzzling Pooch and Pumpkin Puffs

At least they weren't as bad as the ones Matt had bought me for inside. Those I was embarrassed to wear around anyone I didn't know well, because they had multi-colored puff balls on top in pastel colors.

Horridly embarrassing. But they were so comfy…

Anyway. I threw on my outdoor Crocs and as many layers as I could up top and went out to the yard to find where the dog had gone. But because it had snowed there were no prints, so I started a board-by-board check of the fence to see which one might be loose.

That's where Jamie found me. She of course was looking fashionable and adorable in a fur-lined coat that matched her fur-lined boots, her brown hair curled to just below her chin. If I hadn't known that she'd given birth less than six months ago I wouldn't have been able to tell from her slim figure. Some people, I swear, they make the rest of us look bad.

(Still my best friend and love her to death. I'm just sayin'. Some people make it look easy when it is most definitely not.)

"Maggie? This doesn't look like bed rest."

She had Max in his carrier. He was sound asleep like the perfect angel he was, his long black lashes visible against his plump little cheeks. I spared him a quick coo and waved her off as I finished my fence inspection.

"Oh, the Mayo Clinic thinks bed rest is a crock anyway."

"What are you doing?" she asked, running a hand through her curls to fluff them back up.

I shook my head. There she was, the mother of a newborn, and you couldn't even tell. No frizzy hair. No bags under her eyes. I'm pretty sure she was even wearing makeup.

Meanwhile, I hadn't even given birth yet and I couldn't quite remember the last time I'd taken a shower. I was pretty sure it was the day before, but maybe not. And there was a stain on my shirt that was *probably* from breakfast but could've been there for longer.

It was the second (?) day I was wearing that shirt. (Maybe the third? No. Not the third...I didn't think. Although it was possible. Eek.)

Fancy who'd been sprawled in a snowbank taking a nap started in Max's direction, but I called her back to me.

I knew she wouldn't do him any harm, but no one wants to wake up to a big black furry head in their face either. And I was pretty sure Fancy wouldn't enjoy when he grabbed at an ear or a lip. Babies are curious. They explore their world through touch. And putting things in their mouths.

Last thing we needed was Max to try to eat Fancy's ear. Or to get a handful of her slobber. Ew.

"I had a visitor last night," I told Jamie as I led the way inside.

"A bear?"

"No, not a bear." I filled her in on my midnight panic as I made us some tea.

She offered to make it, but I waved her off. I wasn't ready to sit down just yet. Being comfortable was not easy at that point in my pregnancy and in that moment standing felt better than I figured sitting would.

I described the dog for her. "You don't know who he belongs to do you? If so I could at least call and make sure he got home okay. Or let them know I'd seen him here last night if he's still missing."

She shook her head. "No. But...Let me see your laptop for a minute."

Her fingers flew across the keyboard as she muttered to herself. "No. Not that. No. And why are there so many ads on this site? Go away."

"You're starting to sound as cranky as me. Still not getting a lot of sleep I take it?"

She shook her head. "You just wait. With two of them you may never sleep again."

"You know, I was thinking I might just share one of them out to someone else for the first year or so. Maybe Evan and Abe would like the practice until their kid is born?"

She frowned at me. "You're not funny, Maggie. And one day someone is going to think you mean it and you'll be stuck in interviews you don't want to have."

I took a sip of my tea. "I know. But this is how I handle stress. I joke about it."

"Ha! Here it is. Was this him?" She turned the laptop in my direction.

On the screen was a picture of a young couple crouched down with a multi-colored fluffy mutt, his tongue lolling out of his mouth.

"I think so. Who are they?" I quickly scanned the article she'd found. "Oh, that's not good. They're missing?"

She nodded. "Yeah. Went backcountry skiing with their dog, but no one knows exactly where they went and their car hasn't been found so no one knows where to search. And since there were a few avalanches this weekend...Well, it's not looking good."

I scanned the article for more details. They'd been missing for two days already and the family thought they'd disappeared near Breckenridge, but weren't certain.

"How far do you think a dog can travel in two days? Not that far, right? I mean, Breckenridge to here? With mountains in between? And in the winter? It's not like dogs take the highway."

She typed some more and showed me a map. It was almost two hours by car. Could a dog really travel that far on foot? He'd have to climb a couple mountains or find a way through a few snow-filled valleys. And I'd watched enough of those lost in the wilderness shows to know that when you don't know the path you don't always get it right the first time, which would mean lots of false starts and backtracking.

Hm.

I shook my head. "I don't think they're in Breckenridge if their dog is here. I bet they used one of those trails up behind the ski resort. Can you pull that up?"

It took a few minutes, but Jamie finally found a map of backcountry hiking trails.

I leaned forward. "Where do you think people park to reach those trails? Maybe here or here? I bet no one goes up there this time of year...Which means...If we..."

"No."

I stared at Jamie. "No, what?"

"No. You, a heavily-pregnant woman who is supposed to be on bed rest and I, a woman with a newborn, are not going to go out and try to find this couple's car on some remote back road that isn't used in the winter."

"It's not like we're going to try to hike into wherever

they're stranded. I just want to drive up a few roads and see if we can find their car. According to that article they're looking near Breckenridge which is all wrong if that's their dog I saw, which I'm pretty sure it is. Without us they may never be found."

"No."

"But…"

"No."

I glared out the window, regretting that we'd very deliberately chosen not to bring my van to the cabin so that I wouldn't be tempted to drive.

I bit my lip. "They're looking in the wrong place."

"Then we call and tell them."

I rubbed at my belly, feeling a little heel poke into my palm. (Which really is kind of cool when it happens.)

"We could call. It's just that…"

That was boring. And then I'd have to watch it all play out on the news while I was stuck in bed being fat and awkward.

I gave Jamie my best pleading look. "That dog and I have a bond. It wiggled when it saw me. I think it would come to me if we found it again."

"It ran away from you, Maggie."

"Technically. But I think it was running away from Fancy more than me. I'm sure if we went out there and found it again…"

"No." She stared me down. "Do you *want* to give birth in the woods?"

"Of course not. We never even have to get out of your car."

"Do you want to give birth alone with only me to help on some remote backcountry road?"

I sighed. "Noooo."

Jamie didn't say anything more, just raised her eyebrows and stared me down.

"Can't we just drive around a little bit? Look for signs that someone ran off the road somewhere? I bet they ran off the road after they'd finished skiing. Let their guard down and whoosh, there they went."

"Maggie. Bed rest."

"But Mayo…"

"Mayo nothing. Your doctor ordered it."

I tried to cross my arms but there was too much in the way between my boobs and my belly. "Sometimes doctors are wrong."

"Fine. Let's say that this individual doctor was wrong about bed rest. Science as a whole, though, rarely is. And science says that when a woman is pregnant with twins they're usually early. Which means it doesn't matter about bed rest or not I am not going to drive you into the twisty, turny side roads around the valley looking for a dog and some lost couple. Not when you could go into labor at any moment."

"I am not going to go into labor right now. And Jamie, they have a baby with them. What if…" My mind started to spiral around where they could be and what could be happening and my eyes filled up with tears.

"All the more reason to leave it to the professionals." She closed the laptop with a definitive snap. "Now. Let's talk about what really brought me here. I brought you more pregnancy ice cream to try. Sriracha and plum."

She grabbed a small container from the freezer as I said, "Sriracha and plum? What is wrong with you?"

She scooped up a big bite of the ice cream and held it out. "Try it."

I wrinkled my nose. "Do I have to?"

"Yes."

(She was going to make a very good mother with that tone.)

I took a very, very small taste. It was…not exactly bad. Actually, it was kind of good?

"How do you do that? How do you take these weird flavors and make them taste good together?"

She shrugged. "Spicy and sweet work well together."

"But in an *ice cream*? Huh." I took the spoon and container from her, plopped down in a chair, and kept eating. I glanced towards the closed computer. "Jamie…"

"We're not going to drive around trying to find those people. But I'll call it in. There's a number for any tips in that article."

"Fine." It wasn't what I wanted, but it was better than doing nothing.

CHAPTER 7

Jamie called the tip line and told them everything we knew as I continued to eat the surprisingly good ice cream.

"The man on the line was very nice. He said they'd bring a tracking dog by in a little bit to see if they can find a trail to follow."

I scraped the bottom of the container for the last little bit of ice cream. "That's good. Maybe they can at least find the dog today. Poor thing. Out in the cold, alone. I bet he came back and couldn't get inside because Matt blocked the doggie door and now he's probably out there somewhere frozen to death."

Jamie gave me a look. The type that says stop being an overly-dramatic pregnant person. "Animals are smarter than people when it comes to that sort of thing. I'm sure he found somewhere else to shelter for the night. Remember, this wasn't the first day he was missing. He had to have made it through the night before, too."

"Maybe. Maybe he stayed with the family the first night and then they sent him off for help. Like Lassie."

She shook her head as she made another cup of tea. "Would you send Fancy off for help? Because I certainly wouldn't send Lulu off and expect her to ever come back."

I glanced at Fancy who was sprawled on her back against the couch, all four feet up in the air, snoring. "Fair point."

I drummed my fingers on the table. There had to be something more we could do. "Will you do me a favor? And put some dog food out on the back porch, just in case?"

"No."

"Jamie." She'd really taken this whole setting boundaries thing to heart since she'd become a mom. Not that Max was anywhere close to needing those yet. "Why not?"

"You, city girl, did not grow up here. So you have never had a bear in your kitchen. But it happens. Which is why I am not going to put food out on your back porch."

I pouted at her. "But how do we get him to come back if we don't tempt him with food?"

"We could call for him."

"Right. Because we know his name now. You're a genius!" I levered myself back onto my feet. "Come on. We can do it now while we're waiting for the rescue folks."

Jamie and I spent five minutes walking around the backyard of the cabin shouting "Dodger" and shaking bags of treats. But all it did was excite Fancy to the point I had to start shoving treats in her face because every time I shook the bag she'd move to sit in front of me, a small line of drool running from her jowls down her chest.

Our shouts also woke Max from his nap. While Jamie was busy breastfeeding him to calm him back down—she had this under the sweater trick that was thankfully quite unobtrusive—the rescue folks arrived.

The main guy was named Parker and was sexy in a *I wouldn't actually date you because of the facial hair, but I might want to fantasize about you* sort of way.

(What? I was married and pregnant, not dead inside. I can always appreciate a little rugged sexiness.)

But his enthusiasm for our tip wore off as soon as he saw that he was dealing with a new mother and a pregnant woman.

"You're sure you saw this dog?" he asked, holding up the picture from the news. "It couldn't have been another dog that looked like him?"

I threw up my hands. "I'm pretty sure it was that dog. It was the middle of the night. I was a bit startled that some strange dog was in my living room. But, yes, when Jamie showed me that picture this morning it looked an awful lot like him."

"I can't be wasting resources on a dog that looks an awful lot like this one. I need to focus resources where they'll be the most use."

I pressed my lips together. Suddenly Mr. Ruggedly Handsome had morphed into Mr. Know It All Jerk. I glared at him. I bet he'd come over to the cabin so fast because he'd thought Jamie would be attractive. But now that he saw she was a mother with a kid he wasn't interested.

I hate men like that. Who only want to talk to a woman if they think she's attractive. Granted, when you are *not* massively pregnant or carrying around a newborn, that sort of guy can be very useful if manipulated properly.

(Nothing extreme. I'm not a lean on the table and show off the girls sort of person. But a smile and appeal to his kindness can do wonders when a man finds you attractive.)

Of course, it only works if they think you have a certain sort of potential which it seems neither of us did anymore.

(A fact that hit Jamie harder than it hit me. I was eagerly awaiting the day I turned into an old hag that men would overlook. I'd seen enough dirty older men to know that just aging wasn't going to do it, so I was planning on striving for witch in the woods energy when I got old enough. I just had to get Matt on board first which was probably not going to be easy since he'd have to live with me and my rat's nest of hair and saggy clothes and permanent snarl.)

Anyway. Hot ranger dude was not buying my story. But he was already there with the tracker dog so he let the young woman with the dog take a turn around our yard.

"Sorry. I didn't catch any sign. It could be the snow covered the scent." She at least pretended to believe us and for that I gave her my best smile.

"Thank you for trying," I told her. "If the dog comes back I'll try to keep him here this time."

"Good idea."

The ranger dude just rolled his eyes. "Come on. Let's move out. We have a ton of leads to follow-up on today and this one took us out of our way." He shot a nasty look at my belly before walking out the door.

If I'd had the ability to burn literal holes in peoples' backs, he would've been on fire. The young ranger woman gave us an apologetic shrug as she followed him out the door.

After they were gone, Jamie turned to me. "Take a few deep breaths, Maggie. Calm down. *Think of the babies.*"

"Don't even get started with me on that line. Think of the babies. How many times have I heard that in the last couple of months?" But I did take a few deep breaths and sit back down and force all of my annoyance at the ranger dude out of my mind.

Jamie sat down at the table with me. "I'm sure they'll find that couple eventually."

"Yeah, come spring. I mean, really, if you've got a little kid and a dog and you're going to go out for some fun in the snow, why not just join the slew of tourists on the normal ski slopes? Doesn't Winter Park still have that boring-as-can-be trail for cross-country skiers down the backside of the mountain? Why not just take that?"

"It is not boring. It is beautiful. And it's a great trail for cross-country skiing."

I didn't say anything to that. The one time I'd taken that trail it was boring. Then again, I am not a winter sports sort. The closest I get to skiing is hanging out in the lodge with a spiked hot chocolate. And even then I'd rather be curled up at home with Fancy and a book.

Jamie stood up. "Well, I better get going. You're going to rest now, right? For the rest of the day?"

I rolled my eyes and smiled sweetly at her. "Yes, mom."

"Maggie, I mean it. I don't care what some website says about bed rest, you should listen to your doctor. And stop taking on the problems of the world. You've got your own to deal with."

I smooshed my face up at her. "Thanks for the reminder."

"Go on. Go. I'm not leaving until you lie down."

"Really?"

"Really."

I shuffled off to the bedroom. I had every intention of getting right back up after she'd left, but by the time I laid down on my side and arranged my pillow and pulled up the covers and she turned off the light...

I decided a little nap wouldn't hurt. I'd conquer proving that man wrong later.

CHAPTER 8

I woke up to Fancy leaning against the edge of the bed making sad little noises. When I flipped my phone over to check the time I understood why. It was thirty minutes past her dinner time.

"I'm sorry." I rubbed her ears as I tried to force myself awake. They were so velvety soft, I loved them. "Thank you for letting me sleep." I would've kissed the top of her head, but there was a gigantic belly that wouldn't let me bend in half or do anything else for that matter.

Of course, as soon as I moved, my bladder made its needs known, so when I finally did manage to get upright I immediately headed for the bathroom instead of the kitchen, which made Fancy very unhappy. She stood there lecturing me in a high-pitched whine until I was done.

"Sorry, Fancy. But that took priority. Trust me."

She looked at me with the most wounded expression on the planet.

"I know. I know. You did not ask for any of this. Moving cross-country. Changing homes multiple times. Matt. Babies. Murder. Mayhem. I'm sorry."

Her sad but patient look made me feel so guilty I added a couple of Pumpkin Puffs to her bowl. I would've probably given her a spoonful of peanut butter, too, but the vet had informed me on our last visit that Fancy needed to lose weight.

I'd debated having a discussion with him about how research on humans had shown that diets don't really work, but then I realized that I am one hundred percent in control of what Fancy eats and that if I stopped giving her things like treats, peanut butter, and helpings of everything on my plate that she probably would lose weight, so I kept it to myself.

That vet was still a jerk, though. What kind of person walks into the room and immediately says, "It looks like somebody needs to lose weight." Too bad he was the only vet in the valley.

Anyway. To Fancy Pumpkin Puffs were just as yummy as peanut butter, so it all worked out. She was almost done with her dinner when Matt walked in with two pizza boxes.

"There're my girls. All four of you." He kissed my cheek and ruffled Fancy's ears before setting the boxes on the table.

"Four? Oh dear, you're right." I laughed. "You poor man. You're going to spend the rest of your life surrounded by women. Can you handle it?"

"Absolutely."

"And you brought me pizza." I reached for the topmost pizza box. "Have I told you how much I love you lately?"

I opened the box to see a massive heap of sausage, onions, and green peppers. It gave me heartburn just looking at it, and I bit my lip to keep from taking back what I'd just said.

Matt grabbed the box and slid it to the side. "That one is for me. The bottom one is for you."

I opened it. Cheese, tomatoes, and basil. Much better. It probably still wasn't great for me, but I'd take the hit for that yummy melty cheese and crunchy crust. I grabbed a slice and took a big bite as Matt went to the kitchen for plates.

"What did you do today?" he asked.

I told him about Jamie's visit and the ranger who ignored us. "Do you know if they found them yet?" I asked.

He shook his head. "I was swamped all day. Now that the valley's opened back up to tourists it's non-stop craziness."

"Really? Most people haven't even gotten their shots yet."

He snorted. "Like that'll stop a certain type of person who never took it seriously in the first place? And the worst part is that that's ninety percent of the tourists right now, so there's no buffer between the different groups. I never realized how much my job relied on regular, normal people giving a rude look here or there to keep others in check. Now that those folks are hiding away at home for the most part and people are feeling the need to get out and live…It's bad."

"I'm sorry." I gave Fancy a bite of pizza before she drooled a puddle on the floor.

"That's alright. At least the end is in sight. My days of dealing with drunken fools are almost over."

"Are they, though? Because you'll still be dealing with all of that at the pet resort. We all will." I sat down at the table and let Matt serve me up another slice of pizza. "I may not be working the barkery counter myself at the new resort but if I have to stand by and listen to some woman criticizing every single treat in the display case because she wants a discount, I will scream."

I dropped a bite of pizza on Fancy's sharing plate as I added, "I don't like people, Matt."

He laughed. "I know."

"I mean, that's not exactly true. I like you. And Jamie. And my grandpa. And Lesley. And Abe and Evan. And...others who I can't think of right now. But there are so many people in this world I really don't want to be around." I sighed. "Does that make me a bad person?"

"Would you care if it did?" Matt popped open his beer and took a sip.

I gazed at it longingly. I'd never been much of a drinker, but having to give up alcohol for so long made me realize I did like the occasional drink here or there.

I thought about his question for a moment. "No. I don't care. Because I'm still not going to force myself to like that sort of person who's just a jerk. Or so self-absorbed they can't see how they treat others. Or so arrogant they think their you-know-what doesn't stink."

He shrugged. "Well then. Don't worry about it. If it's not going to make you change, worrying about what kind of person it makes you just wastes precious time and energy you could better spend elsewhere."

"Like on finding that poor couple. I can't imagine what they're going through. Do you mind if I turn on the TV?"

"No. Go ahead."

Fortunately, the news was just getting started and the missing couple was the third story. They interviewed the sexy-yet-hairy ranger who grinned at the attractive young reporter before putting on his serious face and turning towards the camera.

"We've focused our search in the Breckenridge area. That's where Zoey's mother thinks they were going. We made progress today, but no sign of them yet. When someone disappears in the backcountry there's a lot of ground to cover, but we're hopeful we'll find them tomorrow."

I set down my pizza and glared at the TV. "I told him they're not in Breckenridge. There's no way the dog could've shown up here if they disappeared in Breckenridge. Stupid man who won't listen to a woman just because she's pregnant."

As I was muttering at the TV they once again showed a picture of the Niels family looking very wholesome and All-American.

"No other leads?" the reporter asked. "Are you sure you're looking in the right area?"

"No. He's not," I said.

"Yes, we're quite sure," he answered. "I mean, obviously, in situations like this you do receive a number of tips from people who want to help and think they've seen something, but we're quite confident they'll be found in the Breckenridge area."

"I saw the frickin' dog!" I shouted at the TV. "I didn't *think* I saw him, I did see him."

"Maggie, calm down."

"I saw that dog. It was here. In this very living room. They are looking in the wrong place."

"You need to be calm. Think about the babies."

I glared at him. If one more person told me what I

needed to do for the babies, I was going to kill someone. And then what was going to happen to the poor babies? Born in prison. Adopted by strangers.

Tell me to think about the babies…Seriously. What else was I thinking about twenty-four hours a day? They had taken over my body like some sort of alien predator. How could I not think about them?

(And yes, yes, it was all so adorable. The sight of a foot thrusting against my skin like some sort of horror movie with a trapped alien trying to escape its fleshy prison. Just adorable.)

I took three deep, calming breaths. For the babies.

"I saw the dog, Matt. I was not mistaken."

He squeezed my hand. "I believe you."

"But they don't. Which means they are looking in the wrong place." I glared at the TV. "He thinks I'm wrong because I'm pregnant and hormonal. *Crazy pregnant lady can't know what she saw.*"

"He could just think you're wrong because you're a woman."

I inhaled through my nostrils and turned to glare at Matt, ready to release all my fury on him, but he was trying so hard not to laugh that my anger fizzled out.

He grinned at me. "It's fun to rile you up sometimes. It's so easy when you're pregnant."

"Matthew Allen Barnes, do not make me divorce you and leave you with custody of our kids."

He chuckled. "Yes, ma'am. I'm sorry. You want some ice cream?"

"Maybe. Did Jamie leave an extra container of that sriracha and plum?"

"Sriracha and plum?"

"Don't look at me, she's the one that came up with it. It's actually really good."

"Huh." He grabbed the container and two spoons. "So now what?" he asked as he took a bite for himself before handing the container over.

"What do you mean?"

"Maggie. I know you. What are you going to do about the missing couple and the dog?"

I took a bite of ice cream before I answered. I knew what my answer would've been before babies and bed rest. I would've been out driving down every one-lane dirt road I could find looking for their vehicle and shouting for Dodger.

But it probably wasn't a good idea to do that. Knowing my luck I'd get stuck on some rutted backroad and go into labor.

"I don't know yet. I was going to put food out so the dog would come back, but Jamie told me that was a bad idea."

"She's right."

"She also said I shouldn't go driving around backroads looking for them."

"Also right."

"But Matt…They're out there somewhere. For the third night. They have to be getting desperate."

He grabbed a handful of cookies out of the panda cookie jar I'd made in ninth grade that was misshaped and poorly painted. I'd brought it with us because (a) we needed a cookie jar and (b) it reminded me of my childhood.

(Matt hadn't said a word about it. Love is living with your significant other's sentimental claptrap, because that thing was fugly.)

He handed me a cookie and sat back down at the table. "Okay. You can't go for a drive or put out food. What can you do from here to help find them?"

I glanced towards the television where they'd now moved on to the weather. Two more days before the next snowfall was expected.

"I wish I knew where they were actually going. How do you go skiing in Colorado in the backcountry in the middle of winter and not tell anyone where you're going?"

(Ignore the fact that I have never once told anyone where I was headed when I went out for a hike. Even in dangerous countries when traveling alone.)

"Good. Go with that. How can you find that out? Sounds like the rangers have already talked to her mom. I bet they've also talked to other family members and neighbors and friends. Who else would know? Where else could you find that information that they haven't already looked?"

I thought about it as I nibbled on the cookie. No friends. No family. No access to phone records. Or email. But…

"Social media. If either one of them had an account, maybe they said something about it. I know more about some people's personal lives because of what they post online than their family does."

"There you go. Track it down. Find their accounts. See if there's a clue about what they were planning."

"But shouldn't the cops have already checked that?"

He shrugged one shoulder. "Only so many hours in the day and so many available resources. If the family is saying Breckenridge and the first few posts don't say anything different, they might not have dug deeper. Or they might have stopped at Facebook and never found Twitter or a blog."

I nodded. "Okay. Makes sense. Thank you. For humoring me."

He kissed my cheek. "I'm not humoring you. You're a force to be reckoned with when you set your mind on something. And I want to see that family found just as much as you do." He stood up. "In the meantime, now that I'm home, we can leave the doggie door open and see if Dodger comes back."

I blew him a kiss as he walked towards the back door. "I love you."

"Come here and give me a real kiss then." He winked at me.

I was tempted. He's a good-looking man. But...

"Sorry, I love you, but I do not love you enough to move from exactly where I am right now. Nothing hurts, the babies aren't kicking, and I don't have to pee. I am going to hold on to this state of bliss for as long as I possibly can."

I batted my eyes at him. "Which means I need you to go get my laptop, please."

"Yes, ma'am. Will do. And then I'm going to grab my service revolver from the lockbox in the car. Just in case we do attract a bear or mountain lion."

"No. No guns in the house. Ever."

"Maggie...Be reasonable. What if whatever comes in that doggie door isn't a dog?"

"Then you find some other way to deal with it. Look. I trust you. I love you. But the statistics are the statistics. No gun in any house I live in. Ever."

He frowned at me. "You can sleep with a knife on

your bed stand, but I can't sleep with a gun in the drawer?"

"Exactly. I am very unlikely to in any way harm anyone with my knife even if I need to. But a gun?" I shook my head. "Too easy to use."

"I am trained, you know."

"I don't care. Chalk it up to my mom's pacifist nature that she passed on to me. No guns in the house. Especially not for the next eighteen years."

"You're being silly."

I shrugged my shoulders. Maybe I was, but that was one topic I was not going to cave on. Ever.

He pursed his lips. "Fine. But I am going to put my baseball bat near the bed."

"Feel free. Now can I please have my laptop so I can get to work?"

As Matt grabbed the laptop for me I realized that was probably as close as we'd ever come to a deal-breaker kind of fight. Odd all the little landmines that exist in a relationship that you never see coming until you step on them. I was just lucky he let it go, because I wouldn't have, and I did not want to do this whole babies thing on my own.

CHAPTER 9

Lucky for me, Zoey Niels lived her entire life online. I swear that woman didn't take a bite of food that wasn't posted to Instagram or Facebook or both. And the videos on TikTok…Oh my.

That woman had cutesy opinions about everything. And little hacks for how to clean this or repair that. (Walnuts to fix scratches in your cabinets? Who knew.)

And the lunches she made for her husband? Hm. Let's just say I didn't let Matt see those. Loved him, but I was not going to hand-draw love notes for him every day of his life while putting gourmet food into little cutesy containers. The 50's ended for a reason, thank you very much.

It was wild. But the real substance was on her blog.

She posted every single day. Even when all she had to share were pictures of her sleeping child. Every. Single. Day. That woman did not miss.

I was in awe of her dedication. I knew more about her life after three hours than I did about the lives of my three best friends combined, and I was married to and living with one of them.

A Puzzling Pooch and Pumpkin Puffs

"Find anything useful?" Matt asked after he'd finished watching whatever hockey game had been on.

(I don't watch hockey. To me the Avs are that team we bought from Canada so we could win whatever trophy you win when you're the best hockey team in North America. They aren't a *real* Colorado team like the Broncos. And, yes, I realize how absurd an opinion that is since they've been in Colorado for twenty-plus years, but it's still the way I feel about it.)

I stared at the notes I'd taken before answering him. "Depends on what you think is useful. I know her food allergies. I know she struggled with postpartum depression and that it freaked her out because she'd dealt with some serious depression in college. I know the names of all of her dogs, ever, including the one she had when she was two years old. It was a golden retriever. I know that Dodger was a rescue they adopted last year. I know that she one day wants to go to Paris. And that she's written a novel. But none of that is going to help find them."

"Nothing about where they were headed then?"

"Nope. Just a mention that she was feeling a little stir-crazy and wanted to get out and that maybe it was time to try some backcountry skiing. I guess they'd done it a lot before the baby came, but not since."

"Where did they like to go?"

"No idea."

It's crazy how someone could live that much of their life online and still not mention something so obviously important. Just goes to show, that even when you think someone is sharing *everything* about their life, that they're really not. There is no substitute for a good face-to-face conversation.

"Could there be another blog?" He sat down across from me and pulled my notes over to scan through them.

I shook my head as an uncontrollable yawn overtook me. "Maybe? Probably. I went back six months on all of her socials, but it looks like I'll have to go back even further. Ugh." I set the laptop off to the side. "Tomorrow, though. I am wiped out."

"You don't have to do this, you know. It's enough to be working on the resort and taking care of Fancy and being pregnant. You don't have to try to find a couple of complete strangers."

"I know. But...I feel obligated."

He raised one eyebrow. "Because the dog found you?"

"Exactly. And I can't just leave it alone now knowing that they're looking in the wrong place." As I stood up and shuffled towards the bathroom, I asked, "Can we drive around tomorrow? Just a little bit?"

"Maggie..."

"I'm not going to go into labor. I promise."

He laughed. "I don't think that's something you can promise. Especially when the doctor has already put you on bed rest and twins come early."

I gave him my best winning smile. "Worst comes to worst, you can deliver the babies, right?"

He laughed, a full-throated roar of amusement. "No."

"But you're trained in emergency situations."

"I am not about to try to deliver my own children. I would be too nervous. About you. About the babies. No. Not going to happen."

"Right. Because I'm not going to go into labor unexpectedly. But if I did...You could handle it. I have faith in you."

He came over and kissed my forehead. "No."

I sighed deeply. "Fine. I guess we just sit around and hope that Dodger returns then."

"I guess so."

I gave him one last glare before I toddled off to the bathroom. It was good I'd married a stubborn man. But there were moments…

CHAPTER 10

I woke up in the middle of the night and struggled out of bed, careful not to step on Fancy who was sleeping pressed up against the side of the bed mere inches away from me. I had to be careful as I scooched down the bed and moved around her to not step on that one back paw she sprawls out from her body. You can never see it, but it's lurking, just waiting to be stepped on.

Pre-pregnancy it was easy to maneuver around her, but almost eight months into my pregnancy, not so much. Somehow I managed, though.

The whole time I was shuffling around and getting up, Matt snored away contentedly on the other side of the bed. My big, brave protector.

I swear, he'd sleep through an earthquake. Fancy on the other hand is always on a hair-trigger where I'm concerned, so her breathing immediately shifted from deep, deep breaths to alert and poised to act.

"It's okay," I told her. "I just need to pee."

But of course Fancy doesn't understand English or the concept of time quite as well as I'd like. So my getting out of bed was the equivalent of "time to be up" in her world. Anything within about three hours of normal wake-up time means she's up and ready to go and expecting attention.

I tried to get her to go back to sleep, but she stood in the living room and cried softly at me until I finally threw on a heavy winter coat and stepped outside into the cold, cold night air with her. I wasn't letting her out alone in the middle of the night, not after all that talk of bears.

It was peaceful out there. I could see the shape of a few of the other cabins amongst the trees. Somewhere an owl hooted. But other than that it was just me shivering on the porch and Fancy crunching through the snow as she went to pee.

It was dark out there. Darker than I ever remember it being in DC or Denver. Light pollution they call it. Big cities are always too lit. But up in the mountains, tucked away on the back corner of a resort, that was not an issue. It was so dark Fancy blended right in. My little spot of blackness in the blackness.

I heard a rustle somewhere off to the side.

"Come on, Fancy. Come back inside," I called.

No response. Knowing Fancy she'd laid herself down in a snowbank. Forget that it was cold enough you could see your breath. This was her happy place. Silent, cold, dark. Outside.

It was not mine.

"Fancy. Come on. Come back in. It's the middle of the night."

Still nothing.

I didn't know where a flashlight was or if we even had one to use. And I wasn't about to go stumbling around in an unfamiliar yard trying to find her. But I didn't want to leave her out there either. All that talk of mountain lions and bears had made me a little paranoid, you know?

I mean on one level I was sure there wasn't some predator out there stalking me or my dog. Bears and mountain lions tend not to want a big hassle. If you're a predator who has to kill to eat, you choose the path of least resistance. Why go after the challenging target when you can find the quick bite instead?

But still.

"Fancy. Come on."

A shuffling noise off to the right made me whirl around. I'd forgotten I was an ungainly beast with a weird center of gravity, so I almost knocked myself on my butt before I managed to grab the railing.

"Fancy? Is that you? Come on then."

Two eyes stared at me out of the darkness.

"Fancy?" I said, softer. Was that really how tall she was? Were her eyes really that big? And did they glow like that when it was dark?

The eyes blinked and whatever it was came one step closer.

I laughed nervously. "Come on now, Fancy. Time to go in. Treat?"

Treats always work with Fancy. And it did that time, too. She came lumbering up from my *left* and looked at me attentively. I nudged her through the doggie door and then slowly turned my head back towards where I'd seen those shining eyes.

They were still there.

"Dodger?" I asked, my voice squeaking higher at the end.

I'd been able to convince myself the eyes might be

Fancy's. Maybe they were a little big and a little high in retrospect, but it was at least possible. Dodger on the other hand…

Yeah, no.

As whatever animal it was took a step closer, I reached for the door handle, still trying to block the doggie door with my body so Fancy wouldn't come back out.

There was a railing around the deck. It would stop whatever it was.

I hoped.

I groped around for the door handle, never turning my back on those very big, very still eyes until my hand finally closed over the handle and I could open the door and step inside. Quickly. Well, as quickly as an ungainly pregnant woman can step.

As soon as I was inside, I slammed the doggie door cover back into place, my heart racing as I tried to look through the window. It was too bright inside and too dark outside to see anything.

I turned off all the lights, but I still couldn't see anything. Hopefully, whatever that had been was gone, but I was not going to take any chances. I wanted to help Dodger but I was not going to leave the doggie door open anymore. No siree. Not at night.

A ripple of pain spread across my belly and I sat down at the kitchen table, taking the type of calming breaths I'd learned during that one summer of Ashtanga yoga. Ujjayi breathing. I figured they'd helped with skydiving panic, they could help with this, too.

But they didn't. My heart was racing. My body hurt. And Fancy was sitting there with a sad look that darted back and forth between me and the treat container.

"Sorry, Fancy. I did promise, didn't I? Just give me a minute here, okay?"

She stared at me with those sad amber eyes of hers. Unblinking. Judging. Demanding. (Sweetly, of course. That's why I always feel so bad if I neglect her in any way. Because she's so accommodating and accepting when it happens.)

"Okay. I think…I think I'm okay now." I shoved to my feet, gave her a treat, and went to the door one more time.

No eyes. Just darkness. Lots and lots of darkness.

"Well, Dodger, I'm pretty sure that wasn't you. And I really hope you don't run into whatever it was."

I made my way back to bed, Fancy at my side. As I snuggled in with my pillow and Fancy sprawled on the floor next to me, Matt continued to snore away softly, completely oblivious to our little mid-night adventure.

CHAPTER 11

The next morning on the news they still hadn't found the missing couple so I went back to my social media snooping. It took some digging, but I finally found a small blog from a few years before that the couple had devoted to hiking and hiking pictures.

That's the thing about the internet. All the information you need is probably there somewhere, but finding it…that's a completely different story.

The blog had only been used for a year right after they started dating and then for some reason they'd abandoned it. The only reason I found it was because she'd linked over to it when she started her new blog. Which had meant going through so, many, posts. Oh my gosh. So. Many.

She hadn't (thankfully) posted on the hiking blog daily. But it did seem to document every single hiking trip they took that year. Not just Colorado either, but Moab, too.

I once went hiking in Moab. We were going to camp out in the wilderness for three nights as part of a school trip. But we couldn't find water. So we ended up at a hotel instead. Which is one of the many times I did not become some tragic story on the news. Glad the teacher wasn't foolish enough to assume we would eventually find water and have us push on.

Anyway. There were about forty posts on the blog, each full of gorgeous photos. The Niels were so young. And happy. And full of energy.

Just looking at the pictures made me feel old and boring. Then again, at their age I'd been spending my weekends shopping or sitting on the couch watching DVDs, so I guess I'd always been boring.

I know that we're all humans and supposed to be alike because of that, but it occurs to me sometimes that humans are as diverse as dog breeds.

Everyone is trying to pretend we're all just "dog" and fit us all into the same little bucket of behaviors and beliefs. But really some of us are Newfoundlands who want to sleep all day and love water and good food, others are labs who want to be out in the wilderness hunting or hiking with their people, some are golden retrievers who love literally everyone and just want attention, and some are Chihuahuas who are full of anxiety and ready to throw down with the biggest baddy around to show they're not actually as scared as they are.

It fascinates me that we all understand those differences when we look at dogs, but then we turn to one another and are like, "What's wrong with you that you don't like almond milk soy protein shakes and going for a run first thing in the morning? You just need to try it and you'll love it."

Yeah, no. Never. But nice try.

Anyway. I digress.

A Puzzling Pooch and Pumpkin Puffs

While I was tracking down her social media, Matt, being the saint he is, made me yummy breakfast frittatas.

They're not really frittatas in my opinion because they go in a muffin tin and frittatas are flat, but that's what the recipe called them, so that's what Matt called them, so that's what I reluctantly call them, too.

Whatever they were, they had all the yummy goodies you want in a breakfast. Eggs, ham, cheese, spinach, and mushrooms.

Okay, so maybe you don't want that in your breakfast, but I did. Pair that with some hashbrowned potatoes, an apple, and some orange juice and you've got a good meal. Oh, and salsa. Never forget the salsa.

Matt even did the dishes when we were done. But then he had to leave for work.

It took me another hour to parse through all those posts and mark each location I could identify on a map. I was so thorough I even marked every location someone in the comments mentioned. (To be fair, there weren't many. That's the sad fact of social media. Lots of great content out there, but most people have five followers or less and that's including family.)

When I was done I spread the map out on the table and stared at it, waiting for it to reveal its secrets. I don't know what I was expecting. Some great big arrow from on high saying, "Here. Right here. They are here."

That did not happen.

I rarely get lost, but at the same time geography is not my strong suit. So I knew where we were and I knew where all the little marks on the map were, but what I was missing was that sense of how they fit together. Which of the spots on the map were close enough to the valley geographically for them to have gone to and for Dodger to have then made his way to my cabin.

I had no clue.

Luckily for me, my grandpa dropped by before I could tear the map up in frustration.

"Maggie May, what are you doing out of bed?" he asked as he opened the front door.

"You could knock you know," I told him as I stood up and went over to kiss his cheek.

He'd aged in the last two years since I'd moved to the valley. He still looked twenty years younger than he was with his faded brown hair and flannel shirt and jeans. But there was more weight on his shoulders.

He was happy, don't get me wrong. But life's hard, you know? Bodies wear down. And the world was…a lot.

Not just the lockdowns and fear about getting sick, but that January mess had really thrown him for a loop, too. We didn't talk politics because I still wanted to love him and certain beliefs and behaviors get so ingrained you can't argue them away easily, but I figured he'd voted for a certain person and seeing that January thing made him finally realize that maybe that person wasn't who he thought they were.

The world he'd grown up in—which had not been an easy world as evidenced by the time he spent in prison because he'd been too poor to think of any other solution to life than bank robbery—had changed.

And I think he knew it wasn't going to change back.

That comes with a certain dose of fear. And a feeling like, *I am too old for this, I do not have it in me to adapt to whatever THIS is.* Heck, I wasn't even forty yet and *I* felt that way.

But he was still there despite it all. Carrying on, holding his head up high, and keeping all the rest of us on our toes.

He took off his jacket and hung it by the door. "If I knocked you'd just run off to bed so I wouldn't know you were disobeying doctor's orders."

I laughed. "I'm afraid running is beyond me these days. Coffee?"

"Sure. You sit. I've got it." He made his way towards the kitchen. "Easy enough to pop one of these little things in the machine."

He took a minute to figure it out, but he managed.

"So what brings you around?" I asked.

"Mason asked me if I could do a bit of woodwork in the reception area. He wanted some flourishes to make things look fancy."

"Oh."

I pursed my lips. It seemed Mason and I needed to have a bit of a chat. I didn't mind him including my family in the resort, but it would be nice to know when he was going to do so. "Let me guess. Does he have Jack working around here, too?"

(Jack is Matt's brother, a reformed hellion with too much charm for his own good. But he's a good general contractor and maintenance guy.)

"As a matter of fact. Jack is doing the base work and then I'm doing the fancy work. Problem?"

I shook my head. "No. I'm glad he's using you guys. I just wish I'd known. It seems odd is all. Didn't he have anyone else he could call?"

My grandpa plopped down in the chair opposite me. "You spent too much of your life in the big city. Here there are only so many choices when you want something done. Plus, why wouldn't you call on the people who are friends and family?"

I thought about it for a second and winced at my answer. "It's harder to yell at friends or family if the job isn't done well."

He leveled a look at me that made me feel two inches tall before pointing his chin at the map. "What's this mess you've got spread out on the table here?"

I told him about the dog that had been in the cabin and the missing couple and how I was sure they were near us but how the rangers thought they were in Breckenridge. And I showed him her blog and the map I'd put together from it.

"Hmm." He studied the map. "It's possible if they went to one of these three locations here that are north of Breckenridge that the dog could've made his way along here and reached the valley."

He tapped his finger on the map and sat back. "But not likely. Are you sure the dog you saw is this couple's dog?"

"Grandpa."

"It was the middle of the night. You were wound up. You didn't have the picture with you at the time. Are you certain it was the dog?"

"What other dog could it be?"

He shrugged and took another sip of his coffee. "I don't know. Lots of cute fluffy mutts that look alike out there."

I felt tears starting in my eyes.

"Now, now, Maggie May. No need to get upset. Come on now." He brushed a tear off my cheek.

"It's just…" I sniffled. "I hate this. I hate not being able to do things. And…being forgetful. And tired. And having people not listen to me anymore."

I stared at a small scratch on the table and ran my finger over it. "And worrying that I'm going to screw it all up once the kids are born. I don't think mother instincts just kick in like everyone wants you to believe they do. What if, what if I'm a bad mother?"

He squeezed my hand. "You are not going to be a bad mother. Look how you are with Fancy. And you had some of the best parents around to set a good example. And that man of yours is a good man, too. Plus you have a whole community that will support you when you need it. You'll be just fine."

Fancy came over and leaned against my chair and I ruffled her hair as I sniffed and tried to control myself.

My grandpa leaned closer. "It's okay to be scared. We all are at one point or another. The key is to not let the fear shut you down."

I nodded and stared at the map once more. "Maybe you're right. Maybe it wasn't Dodger I saw. In which case…" I spread my hands apart in defeat. "I just wasted an entire morning on some stupid map that no one needs."

"Tell ya what. I have a few friends who are rangers and involved in this search. Let me reach out to them and share what you put together here. Even if the dog you saw wasn't that couple's dog, that doesn't change the fact that you've identified some likely spots to find them." He lifted my chin. "Sound good?"

"Yeah, I guess."

"It wasn't wasted time, Maggie May."

I nodded, reluctantly.

"Now. You go lie down for a bit and rest."

I rolled my eyes. "I'm so tired of resting." (And yet, a good nap sounded kinda nice right then.)

"I know. But I need enough time to finish that crib for you so you can't go into labor just yet, you hear me?"

I nodded. "Okay. I'll do it. For you."

"Good." He kissed my cheek and took his cup to the kitchen while I shuffled off to sleep, yet again.

CHAPTER 12

I woke up from my nap just in time for the twelve o'clock news. Fancy of course really didn't care that the news was on or that there might be a story I wanted to watch. She had patiently slept next to my bed for most of the morning and now wanted to go outside.

She picked up her stuffed snake with all the squeakers and took it to the front door.

"I can't, Fancy. I'm sorry."

I was willing to push the doctor's orders a bit, but not enough to take my dog for a walk. Fancy's a good walker, don't get me wrong, but when a hundred and thirty-five pounds of dog wants to chase a squirrel or cross the street to say hi to another dog, that requires strength to hold her back. And balance. The last thing I needed was to lose control of her and fall and go into labor and…

No.

"I'm sorry. I am. Come on. We'll go out on the back porch."

The small cluster of cabins with fenced in yards on the edge of the resort property had been one of my brilliant ideas. I loved to travel before I got Fancy but afterward it became much trickier.

Staying in a hotel room with a dog is always a bit hit and miss. There was the time the room didn't have carpet and Fancy wouldn't set more than a foot inside. And the time we had to use an elevator. And that really long hallway with multiple barking dogs behind doors that scared her so bad she wouldn't move.

A small little cabin with a fenced-in yard for her to go in and out as needed? Perfection.

I would've paid a premium for something like that when I was traveling with her. I just hoped that others felt the same. If our bookings for the summer were any indication, they absolutely did.

And in these plague times being able to stay in a standalone unit without shared air? Even better.

Fancy dropped her toy on the floor and followed me outside. If she'd been a toddler—which dogs kind of are—she would've been dragging her feet the whole way and pushing out her lower lip in a disappointed pout.

"I'm sorry. I am. I know I keep saying that, but I really am."

I could just imagine what she was thinking. *Fat lot of good saying you're sorry is when you still go ahead and do whatever it is anyway. Just like when you tell me you love me as you do something I really don't like you to do, like trim my nails.*

Sigh. Puppy parenting is hard. *Life* is hard.

Fortunately, Fancy can always be brought around with a treat or two, so I fed her about five Pumpkin Puffs and then she was content to lie down on the porch in the shade.

I sat in the sun, because it was frickin' cold out. I also wrapped myself in the big heavy blanket I'd pulled out of the closet. That made it just bearable enough to stay out there with her for a little bit.

Since I am completely incapable of just sitting somewhere and doing absolutely nothing, I ran back inside after about a minute.

"I'll be right back," I promised Fancy, because otherwise she'd follow me.

As I grabbed my laptop and a cup of tea I continued to tell her that I'd be right back, it was okay, stay where she was, don't worry. She was alert to the fact that I was not there, but she waited patiently until I returned at which point she gave a deep sigh, closed her eyes, and promptly fell asleep.

As I sipped my cup of tea, I navigated to the website for one of the local news stations down in Denver. I debated between clicking on the linked article about the Niels or just watching the live coverage, and finally opted for the news article.

(It looked like they were covering sports on the live segment anyway which meant it was too late for any of the news that actually mattered.)

(To me. Yes, I know, for some sports are important.)

The news article didn't really say anything new, just that they were missing and people were searching. But just as I was about to click away from the news site and get lost in my email/Facebook/Twitter death spiral for an hour or so, they interrupted the live broadcast with breaking news.

I unmuted my computer and clicked on the video.

"This just in. Authorities have located Zoey and Trevor Niels. The Niels, their baby, and their dog are all safe. We go live now to the scene."

The footage cut away to one of the fresh-faced newbies the station had recently hired. I know the old-school anchors who've been there forever, but I can never keep track of all the shiny new faces who will soon leave for jobs in Miami or LA or New York or whatever the bigger markets are.

This one was a young woman with dark hair and warm brown eyes and honey-colored skin. She pointed to an ambulance behind her where Zoey and Trevor Niels were seated, paramedics checking them over. Zoey was holding the baby and leaning against her husband. They looked tired but happy.

Their dog was barking and running around their feet. He seemed to have an overabundance of energy.

Fancy heard the barking and lurched to her feet. She ran off into the yard barking in all directions.

"Sorry, Fancy, it's just the computer," I called after her.

I used the distraction as an excuse to go inside where it was actually warm. I should've probably called her in with me, but there was no one around to be bothered by her barking and I was too tired to multitask.

I turned my attention back to the screen just in time to see my not-a-very-nice-guy-after-all-but-still-sexy-in-a-hairy-way ranger step up to give a statement.

He rattled off the details of when they'd found the couple and what state they were in.

It seems they'd been fine on their skiing outing, but then run off the road on a narrow turn as they were headed home at the end of the day. (I knew it.) They'd assumed someone would come by to find them so had stayed in their vehicle, but no one had.

Mr. Niels had spent the daytime hours that first day

putting a bright orange tie on the tree next to where the car had slid off the road and building a big SOS on the ground for anyone doing a flyover to find, but then they'd just hunkered down and hoped.

Fortunately they'd had enough water and food to last for a week.

(You might think they should've tried to get out, but really I think what they did was the best call. It's easy to get lost wandering the woods and end up in a stream or caught out without shelter at night. I once read this book, *Deep Survival,* that was really good and talked all about how adults sometimes have the wrong survival instincts. It's also I'm pretty sure what would explain how they were fine when they were skiing because they knew that was risky, but then ran off the road when the "danger" was past. Maybe not, though. It's been a decade since I read that book.)

The ranger smiled into the camera. "The real breakthrough in this search came this morning when someone who'd taken the time to track down the Niels' old hiking blog gave our rangers a map of all of the locations they'd mentioned. The Niels weren't in any of those identified locations, but it gave our rangers an idea of another location to try. And, as you can see, we sent a team up there, and found them."

I smiled. I had actually helped. Take that Mr. Too Hairy Who Doesn't Listen To Smart Women.

My grandpa opened the front door just as the ranger was finishing his statement. "You're up."

"Just got up a few minutes ago, I promise."

Fancy ran to the front door with her stuffed snake in her mouth and looked imploringly back at me.

I sighed. "I'm sorry, Fancy. I can't. I really can't."

"What're you apologizing for?"

"She wants to go for a walk. But I can't. I sat out on the porch with her for a bit, but clearly it didn't work."

He pressed his lips together. "It's too cold for you to be sitting out there."

"I was fine. But you know what would really help me…" I batted my eyes at him. "If someone were to take Fancy for a walk. She really loves you, you know."

"You want me to walk the dog? When she has a perfectly good backyard right there?"

"It's not the same." Fancy and I both looked at him, begging. "Would you? Please? It doesn't have to be far. Just a little walk. Just down a trail or two."

He frowned down at Fancy as she stared up at him, all patient hope. "Fine. But I came over here for a reason. They found that couple."

"I know. I just saw it on the news. Thank you. For giving them my map."

"Happy to do it. You saw that the dog was with them?"

I nodded.

"And?"

My shoulders slumped. I hate being wrong. "And it wasn't the dog I saw the other night."

"So there's still a mystery to solve then. Assuming you did see a dog."

"I did, see a dog. I am not losing it that much. It was in the living room. I promise you it was a real, live, flesh and blood dog."

"Well, then. You'll have to figure out whose dog that was, won't you?" He winked at me and I smiled back.

"I will. After lunch. You want some? Leftover pizza."

He nodded. "Love to. Right after I walk this mutt. And maybe we can play some Scrabble. I brought it with me."

"Sounds good."

Fancy wagged her tail as she stood at the door and patiently waited to get leashed up.

I rubbed at my belly and smiled as I watched them, realizing how much better my life was now than it had been five years ago.

It wasn't perfect, nothing ever is. But all in all? I had it pretty darned good and was definitely glad I'd thrown my old life away.

(No matter how much I might sometimes worry that I'd made a giant bank-account-emptying mistake. What was money next to family and Fancy, right? Right…)

CHAPTER 13

Of course, me being me, that pleasant little interlude of contentment lasted about five minutes and then I was back to picking at everything in my life that wasn't perfect.

Like that dog I'd seen.

Clearly it hadn't been the dog that belonged to the Niels. But that meant it was someone else's dog. And that it was running around loose in Colorado in the winter. Although, maybe it had found its way home? It didn't look particularly neglected so it hadn't been lost for long, maybe it had wandered away for a few hours and then wandered back.

I wanted to pace the living room while I thought things through, but have you ever been pregnant? Have you ever had ankles so swollen they hurt? No socks are comfortable. None. But I couldn't go without something covering my feet either because it was Colorado in winter and I'm not a particular fan of chilblains.

So I lay down on the couch, tucked the big blanket around my feet, and stared at the floor while silently giving thanks that the cabin was new and I didn't have to stare at some gross stain that would make me worry about black mold or what the prior occupants had done while they were there.

I closed my eyes. The dog was probably fine. It had probably found its way home. (Or already been caught by whatever that big scary thing in the yard the night before was.)

I yawned.

I could let it go. I had babies to worry about. I needed to focus on resting up, staying calm, and letting my body do this crazy weird thing where it took a couple little bundles of cells and turned them into living, breathing people without any conscious effort on my part.

But...

You know me. I can't leave well enough alone. I needed to know about that dog.

Which meant I was going to have to brave the wilds of Nextdoor, that lovely neighborhood forum where people show their weirdness.

I'd once lived in a neighborhood where the posts alternated between "please stop setting off fireworks" and "please keep your stupid dog from barking". Hmm. Wonder what those two things had to do with one another.

But Nextdoor in the Baker Valley was something else. It was usually nature photos, like "see this beautiful deer in a meadow", followed by hunting posts, like "see the buck I got last weekend", with the occasional hot-headed debate over things like fence lines and private property thrown in for spice.

It was a place to start, though. I could check if anyone had posted about a missing dog. And then I could call animal control and the pound, see if they had any reports or had found the dog already.

First, though, lunch with my grandpa. He and Fancy returned about twenty minutes after they'd left looking all red-cheeked (him) and happy (her).

"Good walk?" I asked.

My grandpa grumbled but I could see he'd enjoyed himself. As we ate lunch we talked about Lesley's family and the upcoming t-ball season and everything normal. It actually felt like the world was returning to what it was before, but there was that lingering question of whether we'd really manage to turn the corner or not.

Rather than think about that, which would not be good for my stress levels, I turned my attention back to the missing dog.

"Hey, Grandpa?" I asked. "After lunch will you drive me around?"

"Where? The store? I can pick up whatever it is you need."

"No. Just around the resort. We didn't bring the van so I don't have a vehicle or else I'd do it myself."

My grandpa gave me one of *those* looks. "Maggie May…"

"It's winter, Grandpa. And somewhere out there is a cold, lost dog. I can't put food out for it because everyone tells me that might attract a bear. I can't walk around looking for it because…you know. I can call the pound and animal control and check Nextdoor, but if they don't have anything, I want to go look around. Please?"

He shook his head.

"Grandpa!"

I was not used to being told no. (Actually, people told me no all the time, it's more that I was used to being able to work around them and do it anyway. One more annoyance of pregnancy if there weren't enough already.)

He shook his head again. "Sorry, but Matt would never forgive me for that one. Sometimes you have to be protected from yourself."

"It's just driving around in a fricking car."

"On icy or snow-packed roads. And is that really restful? Would your doctor be happy to hear that you're driving around in the middle of winter looking for a dog?"

"The Mayo Clinic…"

"I don't care about the Mayo Clinic. I care about what your doctor told you. Now, if you want some company I will stick around and we can play a few games of Scrabble before I head back home. But I am not going to drive you around looking for a dog that may not even be lost. Your call."

I pressed my lips tight together. Being pregnant was so damned inconvenient. I was too frickin' selfish for this nonsense. I wanted control of my bladder and my ligaments and I wanted my time back already.

(I didn't want the babies to actually come out yet, of course. I wasn't a fool. I just wanted to somehow miraculously fast-forward to the end already.)

I took three deep, calming breaths. "Fine. Fine. Let's play Scrabble. Who cares about some poor, lonely lost dog out there on its own."

My grandpa didn't say anything, just shook his head and went to grab the Scrabble board.

CHAPTER 14

After my grandpa beat me at Scrabble twice and left, I made my calls. It felt weird, calling to ask about a dog that wasn't even mine, but I had to know.

Neither animal control nor the pound had received a missing dog report and they hadn't seen the dog either. Animal control promised to keep an eye out for it. So did the girl at the pound.

"If you find him, will you call me and let me know?" I asked her.

"Uh, yeah, sure, I guess. But it's not your dog, right? Why do you want to know?"

"So I can stop worrying about it."

"Oh. Guess that makes sense."

"Plus, if you do find it and no one else claims it, I…" I paused for a minute. Did I really want to say what I was about to say? I'd only seen the dog for half a minute and Fancy was probably not going to like it, let alone Matt.

But, yeah, I kind of did. "I'd be interested in adopting it. If you can't find someone else, of course, or the original owners, obviously."

She perked right up at that. "Right. Of course. We'll

absolutely let you know. In the meantime, if you're looking for a dog..."

"I'm not. I'm very pregnant with twins. The last thing I need is another dog."

"But you just said..."

"I know. And in this one particular case, if you find this particular dog, and if you can't find its owner, and if no one else wants it, well, then...I would probably adopt it." I winced, thinking how that conversation was going to go over with Matt.

"Ok-ay..." the girl said, clearly thinking bad things about my mental health.

"Look. Chalk it up to pregnancy hormones, alright. Just call me, please, if you find the dog? Even if you find the owners. Just let me know it's safe."

"Yeah. Sure. Will do. Buh-bye now." She hung up.

I hate being written off as some sort of crazy person. I was going to have to call daily if I ever wanted to find out about the dog.

Then again, to be fair, I kind of was crazy. What was I thinking saying I'd maybe adopt that dog? I had enough going on in my life, I did not need to add a rescue dog to the mix.

I mean, all dogs are great. All of them. But adding a new dog into the house. One with an already developed personality and training and everything else? That's... hard.

Fancy was so good with her sharing plate, but I'd once had a dog her size when I was growing up that would jump up on the counter and snatch a roasted chicken if you weren't careful. And some dogs chew things up. Or bark incessantly. Or have separation issues.

What was I thinking wanting to add a new unknown into the mix? Especially with babies on the way?

Ah well, it didn't matter. I was sure that dog had owners that it had already found its way back to or that would come and pick it up from the pound as soon as it was located. Which meant I was not going to be springing a new dog on Matt at the same time I sprang two babies on him.

It was just words. Meaningless words.

It was fine. Really.

But I did want to find that dog. And I was not going to rest until I did.

Or so I thought. I laid down for just a few minutes to take some of the pressure off my back, fell asleep, and didn't wake back up until Matt came in the door three hours later.

Too bad you can't bank sleep in one period of your life for when you need it in another period of your life, huh?

Alas. None of that sleep I managed pre-delivery was any help post-delivery.

When he came home Matt gave me a kiss on the forehead first thing and gave Fancy a good ear rub. He held up a snazzy plastic food container, the type that has a snap-on lid with an actual seal around the perimeter. "Lesley came into the station today and brought some leftover casserole for dinner."

"Bless that woman. I was not looking forward to a dinner of chips, chicken, cheese, and pickles, which is what we were going to have if she hadn't intervened."

Matt grimaced. "Neither was I. I would've run to pick something up if it came to it. Or we could've had leftover pizza."

"Pizza's gone. My grandpa was here for lunch and I was hungrier than I realized." I slowly levered myself to a sitting position. "I hope you still love me when I'm the size of a house."

"I'll always love you." He helped pull me to my feet.

"You say that now…"

He tilted my chin up and gave me a soft kiss on the lips. "I will say that always. Because what I love about you is that feisty spirit and sharp mind. I mean, don't get me wrong, I like some of the physical things to. Your smile. Your eyes. Your hair…[A few things I'm not going to repeat here for you, dear reader.] But I can't imagine a day will come when you lose every single thing I love about you."

"Well, I can. You need a better imagination."

He laughed. "Maybe, but you need to anchor yourself in the present. Tomorrow will bring what tomorrow brings and nothing that can be done about that."

I rubbed at my lower back. I was so tired of aching everywhere all the time.

Matt handed me the casserole container. "I could use a shower. Are you okay with getting dinner ready?"

I nodded. "Absolutely. But first…" I handed the container back.

"You need to pee."

I nodded. It was a miracle I had any moisture left in my body the number of times I had to pee with those babies those last few weeks.

As I made my way to the bathroom I grumbled to myself about how Matt got to take nice, long, luxurious hot showers anytime he wanted and I was stuck with tepid water until I gave birth. *Tepid.* Miserable. There's nothing soothing or comforting about *tepid* water. The word itself made me want to gag.

I patted my belly. "You two better be worth it, you hear? I want some Nobel Prize-winning efforts out of you." I winced and added, "But, honestly, you can be whoever you want and I will still love you. I promise. Find your bliss."

(Yes, I was a bit back and forth on my parental expectations. I wanted big things from my girls. But I also wanted them to be happy. So I wanted them to live up to their potential while also not pushing themselves so hard they were miserable, anxious, and unhappy all the time. Not too much to ask, was it? Ha.)

As I did my thing I resolved to throw another ten bucks into their therapy fund. They were going to need it with a mom like me.

CHAPTER 15

Dinner was delicious. Some mixture of sour cream and chicken and breading and vegetables. I know a lot of people like that fresh and healthy thing, but for me you just can't beat old-school recipes that involve things like condensed cream of chicken or cream of mushroom soup and a bag of frozen vegetables.

(Although, I am glad the days of my grandma making the frozen vegetables that included lima beans are gone. I have never been a lima bean fan. Ever. Not even when there are equal amounts bacon involved.)

But I digress. (Always.)

Matt and I had finished dinner and I was resting with my head on his lap as we watched some cooking show on the TV when I told him about my day.

He rubbed my shoulder and smiled. "That's my girl. Helping solve a disappearance. You think you'll still get involved in things like that after the babies arrive?"

I sighed. "I don't know. I mean, part of me hopes so because it means my life will not have become consumed by being a mom, worker bee, and wife. No offense. But at the same time, I never really wanted to get involved in half the cases I did, it's just that someone had to. So I kind of hope there aren't any more situations like that. I mean, someone involved in the search for that couple could've easily done what I did."

"Hm."

"What do you mean, hm?"

He thought about it for a minute and I could see he was trying to figure out the right way to frame what he wanted to say. "In my experience, people who are really good at things rarely realize that they're as good at them as they are. I played baseball with a guy in middle school—he moved away after that and made it to the minor leagues, actually—and he used to say things to me like, 'All you have to do is focus on the ball hitting the bat and it's easy to connect.' And for him it was that easy. But for me the ball came so fast I never saw it leave the pitcher's hand before it was in the catcher's glove."

I pressed my lips together. "I guess I get what you're saying."

He chuckled. "No you don't. You're just being polite. So what I will say is this. You have an ability to see what could be done that most people do not. You recognize patterns and put together information that's not even connected as far as the rest of us are concerned."

Before I could argue with that, he added, "To you it's all connected. Just not to the rest of us. I imagine that living in your head is like having one of those conspiracy theory boards with multi-colored lines connecting all the unrelated events to form some bigger picture that no one else believes in until they see what you've put together."

I shifted to make myself more comfortable. "It's not that crazy in here. Anyone can do it if they try. It's just patterns and connections. You hold two things up next to each other and see how they match."

He chuckled and shook his head. "Did you know that there are some people who when they aren't talking or interacting with others have completely blank minds?"

I stared at him. "What do you mean, completely blank minds?"

"I mean that there are some people who when they lie down to go to bed, have nothing in their minds."

"No music?"

He laughed. "No. No music. Which is probably most people, by the way. But also, no thoughts. No memories. No stories they spin to put themselves to sleep. Just…silence."

I sat up. "No! I don't believe it. I mean I met a girl once who said she wasn't thinking of anything at all when she was sitting there quiet, but there can't be more of her in this world than that. Can there?"

He raised his eyebrows and nodded.

"No. I have to look this up."

I tried to find it. I really did. But I couldn't.

"It exists. I promise. People's minds are always functioning because they keep breathing and circulating air and blood and all that, but some people's minds can be absolutely blank otherwise."

I refused to believe him. It just wasn't possible. And I hadn't found it on the internet, which, I mean, the internet has everything.

Then again, I'd once tried to confirm the definition of a heuristic online and had never been able to find a good source for it, but then a year or two later ran across a discussion of exactly what I remembered it to be in a book.

So the internet doesn't always yield its secrets.

Still. No thoughts? None? Just blankness.

I shuddered at the thought.

Matt kissed my forehead. "Regardless. My point is that what you think is easy for others to do maybe isn't. Which is why I suspect that even juggling me and babies and the resort and everything else you will still get drawn into the occasional investigation."

"Maybe. I won't have you as an inside source anymore, though, so chances are I won't even hear about cases except a little blip in the newspaper."

"No, but you'll have an entire pet resort full of interesting mysteries instead. The first dognapping we have, you will be all over it."

I opened my mouth to disagree, but stopped myself because he was right. "Fair enough. Speaking of…"

Matt raised one eyebrow.

"That dog I saw the other night is still missing. I called around to the pound and animal control but they haven't seen it and no one has filed a report."

"It probably found its way back home then."

"Maybe…But."

"You want to track it down."

I nodded. "Can we drive around tomorrow before you go into work? See if it's in a yard near here somewhere maybe? Ask around a bit? It'd really help with my stress levels to know it's safe."

I gave him my most sincere look but he just responded with a look my grandpa would've been proud of. "Maggie."

"Please. Indulge your pregnant wife."

"By risking her health and that of our babies?"

A Puzzling Pooch and Pumpkin Puffs

I frowned at him. I had spent over thirty-five years of my life with no one the least bit concerned about my health, but get pregnant and suddenly my health was everyone's business.

"Maggie. It's winter. You are very pregnant. I know you want to find this dog, but driving down a bunch of small mountain roads looking for it doesn't make a lot of sense."

"Fine." I grabbed my laptop and moved to the table. "Plan B. Or C. Or D. Whatever we're up to now."

"What're you gonna do?"

"A little social engineering, but for a good cause." I opened Nextdoor and typed up a post as Matt watched over my shoulder and read it out loud.

"Hey everyone. Please help me out. I am stuck at home on bed rest and feeling bummed. Will you please post pictures of your favorite furry friends to cheer me up? Let me know names, how you found them, and why they're the absolute best pet in the world. I'll start. This is my girl, Fancy, who has been with me through it all and is right here by my side through this, too. Thanks!"

He shook his head.

I shrugged. "You never know. That dog was adorable. I can't imagine its owner doesn't love it to pieces and wouldn't be proud to post a photo."

"Not everyone is online, you know. Or on Nextdoor."

"True. But what else can I do when my family won't let me leave the house."

He smiled and shook his head. "Do you want ice cream?"

"Does the sun shine?" I flashed him my best smile. "Yes, please. Have I told you you're the greatest husband in the world yet today?"

"No."

"Well, you are."

As Matt went to grab me ice cream (because he really is the best husband in the world), I watched the posts start to come in.

There were an inordinate number of cat photos shared. One lady had six of them and each had its own very unique story. And rabbits, too. Big ones.

Another person shared a photo of a lizard of some sort. Not sure how that qualified as furry, but hey, if it made them happy, which it clearly did, more power to them. Just, you know, read the room, buddy. Soft and fuzzy not scaled and cold, please.

Surprisingly, even though no one had posted about my particular dog by the end of the night, seeing all those cute, fluffy pets and their adoring owners really did cheer me up.

That's the thing with life. There's always going to be some challenge or other or something going wrong, but there's usually also a cute kitten or puppy or beautiful sunrise to balance it out if you look for it.

CHAPTER 16

I'd like to say I slept through the night, but who are we kidding. Between the three trips to the bathroom, the challenge of getting anywhere close to comfortable, and the fact that I was on a hair trigger waiting for that dog (or something else) to come through the doggie door, I did not sleep well at all.

Fancy ran outside barking her head off sometime around two, but when I finally managed to join her outside I couldn't see anything. I knew I should look for the missing dog but I was honestly more worried about the silent predator that had stared me down the other night, so I immediately brought her in, blocked the doggie door, and went back to sleep.

(Yes, it does sometimes take me more than once to learn caution.)

The next morning, after another yummy breakfast courtesy of my yummy husband, I decided to check my Nextdoor post.

And…It was the dog!

Someone had posted a picture of that little fluffy mutt I'd seen that night. His name was actually Spots. He was even more adorable than I remembered. And he had someone who loved him enough to tell strangers about it!

I was all ready for it to be done and over, but then I read what the person had written.

"This is my grandma's dog, Spots. He was there by her side every day for three years and was the best dog in the world. But she lost him on a trip to Denver two years ago. We found him, but that's when we realized she had memory issues. A year ago she needed to go into a care facility and none of us could take Spots, so we gave him to a rescue in Denver who found him a new home. I hope he's out there living his best life. Love you buddy."

I teared up. I really did.

One of my greatest fears is not being able to take care of Fancy for her whole life. No one will love her and care for her the way I do. And think how confused she'd be to suddenly lose her person.

And then to be surrendered to some strange dog rescue. I mean, I know they do amazing work and they mean so well and they really do help dogs, but have you ever been to one of those places? All the cages and concrete and noise?

Fancy would be so miserable.

And she's big, you know? Not everyone wants a big dog. The thought of her just sitting there day after day surrounded by barking, crying dogs wondering what happened that she ended up there...

That's when the waterworks really started.

I was sitting there on the couch, sobbing, Fancy sniffing at my face trying to make it better when Jamie knocked on the door and came in.

(I'm not normally one to just let people walk into my

house, but with the bed rest and all I'd given my grandpa and Jamie permission to come in without knocking. Plus, I was expecting her for a meeting.)

"What's wrong? What happened? Did somebody die?" Jamie rushed to my side.

"No. No one died, at least, I hope they didn't."

Between choked sobs I told her about the post I'd made and the responses and showed her the one about the dog and the grandma. "Isn't that just the saddest? I mean, losing your dog like that. And the poor dog."

"Well, if she couldn't take care of it anymore, it probably was the best thing."

"But to lose everyone you know. How could her family not take him in? And then bring him by for visits?"

"Maybe they had other dogs. Or traveled too much."

I stared at her. I love Jamie. She is my best friend. But we are not identical and our views towards our dogs is one example of that.

Jamie is good to Lulu, don't get me wrong. She pets her and feeds her and gives her treats and takes her places. But at the end of the day Lulu is just a dog to Jamie. Which, fair enough, that's probably the more rational approach to having a dog.

For me Fancy is my partner in crime. She's a living, breathing creature with her own thoughts and feelings that I try to take into account.

I once had her work with a dog trainer after she got scared of going to the groomers, and that guy wanted me to teach her to stare at me our entire walk.

Don't sniff the grass, don't look at other dogs, just watch me for any command I might give.

He wanted to make paying attention to me her entire

world. Which, if you're training a police dog probably makes sense, but I wasn't training a police dog. I was just trying to help my poor dog get over what turned out to be a justified fear.

I handed the guy a check for that session and told him to go away and never come back. For me taking Fancy for a walk is as much about her personal enjoyment and development as it is about mine.

Granted, ultimately my choices are what win out. She didn't have any say in Matt or where we live or the babies. At the end of the day I make the decisions that work for me first and foremost.

But if she'd met Matt and hadn't liked him? No way I would've forced her to share a home with him. And no way I would've given her up for him either, because I took responsibility for her and it is on me to give her a good life.

Not just a "you're a dog so I'll feed you and house you" life, but a *good* life that honors the fact that she deserves comfort, companionship, and enjoyment aside from any pleasure I get from her presence.

So Jamie was absolutely right in what she said about that dog from a practical, reasonable, logical standpoint. But I gave her a death stare anyway.

Because if someone did something like that with Fancy I would've been livid. Or broken-hearted.

But there was no point having that argument. She'd be calm and reasonable and I'd be emotional and hysterical and neither one of us would change our opinion.

Instead, I said, "I bet that dog came back here looking for its owner. She's in a home of some sort now, so he wouldn't find her, but I bet that's what happened."

"From Denver? You said he didn't look that bad."

"Well, I only saw him for a minute or so in the middle of the night."

"Maybe his owners brought him up here and he got away from them."

I nodded. That made sense. "Maybe. Which means they should be looking for him. I wonder…If they brought him up to the mountains, but not the Baker Valley, then they might've called a different pound or animal control looking for him, which is why I didn't find anything when I called the local ones…"

"Easy enough to check, right?" Jamie smiled at me. "This is great news. Now we know he has owners and we can let them know where we spotted him and he'll be reunited with them in no time."

I felt a little sad thinking about that. I mean, I'd literally only seen the dog for a minute at most, but some weird part of my brain had already spun out a tale of us finding him again and adopting him and Fancy getting a friend to keep her company during the upcoming chaos.

Sigh.

At least now the dog had a name. And owners that were probably missing him.

"I need to call around and find out where he was lost. Maybe I can reach out to this person on Nextdoor to find out where they surrendered him. Or call animal control in nearby counties to find out if they've had a report."

Jamie nodded. "Good idea. But first, we have our business meeting."

"Ugh. Right. Business meetings are so much fun. I can't wait."

She laughed and headed to the kitchen to grab some

drinks while we waited for Greta and Mason to arrive. I couldn't believe after all this time that we were mere weeks from opening weekend. There was so much still left to do…

CHAPTER 17

Greta was the next one to arrive, looking as classic and put together as ever. Jamie is always fresh-faced and full of energy so you think she's ten years younger than she is whereas Greta is always so contained and polished you assume she must be ten years older than she is.

I think it's mostly just being a certain type of European. And having a good, classic sense of style. She was wearing an emerald green silk top and black slacks. It worked well with her pale blonde hair and tasteful yet expensive jewelry. I didn't even want to know what the small emerald and diamond earrings she was wearing probably cost.

She kissed me on the cheek. "You are coming along nicely."

"That's one way to describe it."

She patted my hand. "It will be over soon. And then you will wish you were still pregnant."

"Greta, I know it's rude to ask, but with all of your marriages, you never wanted to have kids?"

(Greta had been married something like ten times. Mostly to very wealthy men which had made her very wealthy in her own right.)

She tilted her head to the side. "I have a son. He is twenty. At university in Dusseldorf."

"You have a son?" I looked at Jamie. "Did you know she had a son?"

She shook her head. "Never thought to ask."

"Oh yes. Here. Here is his picture." She showed us a picture of a very handsome young man with a ski slope behind him. "This was taken in Austria on a ski holiday last year."

"He's never been here to visit has he?" I thought we were friends, but maybe I'd been wrong and she'd snuck in a visit with her son without ever mentioning it.

"No. It is…a complicated situation. My seventh husband? He was Spanish. Aristocracy. He wanted my son to go to boarding school. My son was ten at the time?" She huffed. "He was unhappy. He did not like Spain. He did not want to learn Spanish. He missed his friends. So I agreed."

I stared at her. She'd sent her son away to school when he was ten? Rich people are weird sometimes.

"Was that, the last of it? He never came home for the holidays or anything?"

"He would come home in the summer. But when that marriage ended, things were unsettled. My son stayed with a school friend." She shrugged her delicate shoulders. "By the time things were settled and I wanted him to come home, he was thirteen and he did not want to come."

"So you're estranged?"

"No. We talk once a week. And before, I would visit him when I was in Europe, which was often. Or he would visit me." She shrugged again. "We are cordial, but he does not need a mother so much."

I couldn't imagine. If my parents were still alive I'd like to think I'd speak to them more than once a week.

Then again, at twenty maybe I wouldn't have. At that age I had been pretty caught up in my own little world. Still. I hoped my girls were more attached to me at twenty than Greta's son seemed to be to her.

Mason arrived then carrying three large bags of food. He was a good-looking man. Reminiscent of an older but not old Sean Connery. And I'd come around on liking him for the most part. He was a great dad to Max and good husband to Jamie.

Of course, he still sometimes had a stick up his you-know-what. He hadn't changed, I just liked him more than I had initially.

I flashed him a smile. "Mason. I hear you've been hiring all of my family to work for the resort."

"Have I?"

I ticked them off on my fingers. "My grandpa. Jack. My husband."

"Oh. Yes. I have hired all of them." He set the bags of food down on the table and gave Jamie a kiss on the cheek.

"It'd be nice to know you were going to do that before you did it, you know."

He frowned at me. "Why?"

"Because...I don't know. They're my family. Maybe I didn't want that."

He gave me a weird look but didn't answer as he started removing takeout containers from the bags and placing them on the table. "I figured we could sample the food from the on-site restaurants during the meeting."

He glanced at me. "Of course, if I am also not allowed to hire your friends to work for the resort, then I guess we will be starting over and no point tasting the food."

I glanced at the others. "What do you mean by that?"

Jamie patted my hand as she sat down next to me. "Well…You know that Mason and Greta took point on staffing the on-site restaurant."

"Yes."

"As it turns out…"

I glared at everyone. "What?"

"Abe and Evan decided they would like more regular income now that they have a baby on the way, so they're going to be running the casual dining restaurant for us."

"What about the Creek Inn?"

Abe and Evan had been running the Creek Inn just outside the valley from Creek until we shut down the valley by bringing some boulders down across the road just this side of the inn. They'd chosen to close down the inn and move into the valley where there was a better chance of being safe. No point in running an inn at the end of a dead-end road. But I'd always assumed they were going to go back when the valley reopened.

"They sold it. To Sally Broykes."

I looked around the table. This was clearly only news to me. "Why didn't they tell me?"

"When's the last time you saw them?" Jamie asked.

"At the doctor's office when they were there with their surrogate."

"And do you chat with them on the phone? Or otherwise keep in touch?"

I frowned at Jamie. "No. But…"

"Well, then. I'm sure they would've mentioned it next

time they did see you. So that's what these are." She set aside six takeout containers that looked like they had sandwiches or burgers in them. "And these," she pushed three more containers to the other side of the table, "are from the new high-end restaurant that's going to be located up the side of the mountain behind the resort."

"When did we add that?"

She smiled. "When a certain Michelin-starred chef decided to move here."

I threw my hands up in the air. Did I know nothing anymore? "Are you talking about Jean-Philippe? He's moving here permanently? Since when."

Greta smiled serenely. "Since I asked him to. This will be good for the resort, no? Attract a higher-end clientele."

"And you guys? Are you still together?"

She shrugged one shoulder. "We are what we are."

Jean-Philippe had been my freshman-year mistake and Jamie's freshman-year amusement. When he came to rescue Jamie's wedding he and Greta had formed an unlikely connection. As far as I knew his situation with Greta was the longest he'd ever stayed interested in one woman.

"Okay. Wow." I turned to Mason and asked sarcastically, "Is Elaine going to be our accountant?"

"As a matter of fact."

"And Lesley? Did you find a way to rope her in, too?"

"She might be making some pies for us."

I glared at him. "I was joking."

"I know. But I was not. Just so you know, Trish is going to be heading up our housekeeping and Jack is staying on to do general maintenance."

"And Sam?" (He was only nine-years-old, I couldn't imagine they'd found a use for him.)

"Will be around and I am sure will help out from time to time. His parents have permission to bring him to work if needed."

I shook my head. "Good thing Lucas Dean is dead or you would've had him here, too."

"True. The man was a cad, but he was also a very good general contractor."

Without even realizing I was doing so, I'd started snacking on the various containers of food while I glared everyone down. It was good. Really good. Homemade potato chips. Fresh guacamole. Corn salsa. Thick-cut fries with the skin still on.

I shook my head. "I don't like it. Aren't there any other people you could hire?"

Jamie frowned at me. "I don't understand why you're so upset about this."

I tried to think of a way to explain it that didn't sound horrible.

"Look, I love the fact that I'll have everyone I know and like around and that we'll all benefit together if the resort does well. But…I…have been disappointed in the past when I tried to rely on others to do things for me. And I worry that because these people are my friends and family that I won't be able to say anything when they fail at their part of things. I realize that sounds ridiculous, but it scares me to rely on people I like because if they don't come through then I'm not allowed to be angry at them. Or fire them."

Mason popped a fry in his mouth. "I have no problem telling people when they have failed me. Even people I like. Rest assured, I will handle any performance issues just fine." He glanced at Greta as he put some steamed mussels and skinny fries on his plate. "Even my co-investor's lover, if needed." He winked.

Greta raised her chin. "No. *I* will handle any performance issues Jean-Philippe may have myself. I too have no problem telling someone when they have failed me, even someone I like quite a bit. And with Jean-Philippe he is quite used to my corrections."

Jamie laughed. "Well then. If that's settled. Let's talk about the daycare."

"The daycare?" I asked. "I thought we'd already settled that."

"We had. For the pets. But I want to talk about adding a daycare for children. You will have the twins, I will have Max, and Evan and Abe will have their baby soon. Not to mention anyone else who works for us and has a kid too young for school. That's at least five years of having kids to worry about."

She cut a juicy cheeseburger topped with barbecue sauce and onion rings into fourths and took a piece before offering it to me. "As much as I'm okay right now with keeping Max in the back room while I work, I expect he'll outgrow that box of printer paper at some point and also need a little more hands-on management."

"You put Max in a box of printer paper?" That sounded like something I'd do, not Jamie.

She shrugged. "He needed a nap and a box was a better choice than his carrier. So. Daycare? Yes. Where should we put it?"

As they debated the best location for the daycare and whether it should just be for employees' kids or whether it should be large enough to accommodate guests' kids as well, I sat back and enjoyed the food and contemplated where my life had led me.

I couldn't believe my little dreams of what my life would be like living in Creek with my lonely, widowed grandpa and running a small little café and barkery with my best friend had morphed into this. I would've never imagined it the first day I moved to Creek.

My grandpa remarried. Jamie married. *Me* married. Both of us having kids. The resort. Never in a million years.

But there we were. And it excited and scared me in equal measure. It was everything I never knew I wanted, which is why I was so worried that it would be taken away somehow.

Once more I took three deep, calming breaths. (Yes, I was doing that a lot. Because, really, on a daily basis I was about two steps away from needing to breathe into a paper bag.)

Everything would be fine.

Time to take Matt's advice and live in the moment. Life was good *now* and that's all that mattered. No point borrowing trouble from the future. Or so I told myself, but you know me, it didn't work.

CHAPTER 18

After the meeting I took a nap. It's hard creating life. Kudos to every woman who keeps on going like it's nothing until the day they go into labor. I do not know how they do it. I stand in awe.

I have had friends like Jamie for whom pregnancy seemed like this glowy miracle of happiness the whole time, so maybe that's how. But whatever good hormones those women's bodies produced to let them feel that way, mine did not.

So I took a nap with Fancy snoring away at the side of the bed thinking how lucky I was that I had a dog that slept most of the day.

I was sort of drifting in and out of sleep when I heard the doggie door flap and figured Fancy had gone outside. But then I heard her move. Which meant Spots was back!

Or so I hoped.

I dragged myself out of sleep. You know how sometimes if you awake when you're not ready to it's like wading through sludge? It was like that. I sleep best in either three and a half or four hour segments, but this had been something like two hours and I'd been deep in REM sleep and my mind did not want to snap into focus.

When I finally managed to open my eyes Spots was standing in the doorway. Now that I had a better look, he was in pretty rough shape. Pine needles caught in his coat. A bit of a gash on his nose. Mud on his paws.

"Hey there, buddy," I called softly as I tried to sit up.

Unfortunately, my voice woke Fancy and she jumped to her feet as soon as she saw him and he bolted. They both went racing outside as I "scrambled" to follow. I say scrambled because I wanted to hurry after them—the intent was there—but my actual movements were more of an awkward sort of thing where I slowly lurched after them.

By the time I joined Fancy outside, Spots was gone again.

"Spots. Come here, Spots. Come on. Good boy. Come on," I called.

He appeared in the trees a few feet from the fence and Fancy ran over there to bark at him. I swear the only time she has real energy is when she's barking at someone or something through the fence. Even non-pregnant I can't get ahold of her while she's like that. So I ignored her because there was absolutely no chance I was going to corral her as I was.

"Do you want a treat? Let me get you a treat." I went back inside for some Pumpkin Puffs as Fancy continued to run and bark along the fence.

When I came back out she was still barking and he was still lingering there in the woods. As soon as Fancy saw that I had treats, she stopped and turned her attention on me.

"Hey buddy," I said as I approached the fence, holding out one treat for Spots and one for Fancy.

He wouldn't move from his shelter in the trees, so I tossed the treat at his feet. He cautiously sniffed at it and then gobbled it up. Meanwhile Fancy was circling around me trying to get another treat.

"Fancy, stop."

She didn't. Treats are a great way to get her to do pretty much anything but unfortunately that means that she becomes relentlessly focused when she sees them.

I threw all but one of the remaining treats out into the yard for her to find, which bought me about a minute to try to lure Spots closer. He almost came to the fence, but she's fast when she wants to be and was back before I could get him to trust me.

"You stay there, okay? I'll be right back," I told him.

I led Fancy inside with my one remaining treat and blocked the doggie door behind her. She immediately started crying so loud I could hear her outside—she is not used to being blocked away from me—but it was the only chance I had of luring Spots closer.

Unfortunately, he was gone when I turned back around.

"Spots. Come here boy," I called over and over again, but he didn't come back.

I debated following him into the woods, but the pain shooting across my belly warned me that maybe it was time to take it easy.

Sighing, I reluctantly went back inside. At least I knew he was still around. And safe. But I was more determined than ever to find him and reunite him with his owners.

Of course, that meant I needed to know who his current owners actually were.

I stepped back inside, ignoring Fancy's pouting look

of absolute betrayal. She'd laid down two feet from the door in her platypus position (hands sprawled to the sides, chin flat on the ground) and wouldn't take her eyes off me.

"Sorry. But you know I had to do it."

I grabbed my laptop and sat down at the table.

First step was to message the person on Nextdoor who had posted Spots' picture and ask if they'd call me. (Ironically, *I* would not have called some rando who messaged me from Nextdoor, but I was hoping the person was more trusting than I am.)

My phone rang only a few minutes later, showing a call from an unknown number. Which was a bit surprising. I mean, who hangs out on Nextdoor?

"Hello?" I said, waiting to hear about how my car warranty was expired and it was time to renew it.

"Hi. Is this Maggie? From Nextdoor?"

I smiled. "Yeah. Is this Alex?"

I couldn't tell if the person on the other end of the line was a young woman or a man with a high-pitched voice. Didn't really matter I guess, but it's something I think we all try to do subconsciously. Put people into known buckets as soon as possible.

"Yep. You wanted to talk to me about my grandma's dog?"

"I did. I think he's running loose in the Baker Valley. I've seen a dog twice now that looks just like him. We're staying in a cabin on the new Baker Valley Pet Resort property. Is that by any chance near where your grandma used to live?"

"Yes." They suddenly sounded very cold and I wondered what I'd done wrong to upset them.

"Whereabouts?" I asked

"Probably right about where you are now. My parents sold my grandma's place off when we moved her into the care home and those [redacted] developers were going to level it for their [redacted] pet resort."

"Oh. I'm sorry."

I hadn't realized that Mason or Greta had purchased private homes as part of the pet resort development. I obviously knew they'd purchased retail space since the original site of the Baker Valley Barkery & Café had been leveled as part of the work.

That had hurt enough. I couldn't imagine what it would feel like to lose a family home.

Alex answered with a verbal shrug. "Yeah. Well. Nothing to be done about it now is there?"

True enough. And I needed to find that dog, so no point dwelling on it or telling them exactly who I was in relation to the resort.

"So that means Spots came back here but had nowhere to go back to."

"Sounds like it."

They were not warming back up to me, but nothing to be done about it so I just plowed on. "Okay. So if I can find him, I need to reunite him with his owners. What shelter did you leave him at?"

Alex rattled off the information. "That all you need?"

"Actually…While I have you on the phone. If I can't locate the new owners for some reason, would you want him back? In your post you seemed to really love him."

"Can't. I'm at school. No room for a dog. I'm never home. I work two jobs on top of class. And my parents are not dog people. Don't like the mess."

"Okay. Fair enough. Thanks for the information."

"Sure." They hung up.

Not the most pleasant call ever, but at least I was one step closer to locating Spots' new owners. That was a positive. I just hoped they wanted him back.

CHAPTER 19

Before I could make my next call, Elaine stopped by. She'd changed a lot since I first met her that day at the YMCA when I was scoping her out as a potential wedding saboteur. Then, she'd been very plain and mousy and mostly forgettable.

But Jamie had taken her under her wing and taught her a few things about hair and makeup and fashion. She hadn't transformed into some tarted up mess, but thanks to Jamie's guidance Elaine had started using a bit of mascara and some lip gloss and making better fashion choices.

(Me, personally, I am all for the no makeup, sweats for life club, but if you actually have to interact with the rest of the world it is good to know how to present well to others.)

"Hey, Maggie. I hope it's okay that I came by. I was bringing some masks for the resort and Jamie mentioned you were staying here until the delivery."

"Absolutely. Come in."

She stepped into the living room area and glanced around awkwardly, but then Fancy made herself known and Elaine immediately relaxed as she said her hellos to Fancy and gave her a few good chest and chin scratches.

"So you're still doing the accounting?" I said. "I figured after news broke of how talented you were as a dress designer that you'd be quitting your job and taking on a bunch of fancy, high-end wedding projects."

She ducked her head and blushed. "I have had a commission or two, but sewing is what I love. I didn't want to turn it into a business venture. Especially since the Mason Foundation provides very good benefits. Better to be able to pick and choose what I work on."

"Oh, that makes sense. Everyone's so ready to rush to turn their passion into a business it never occurs to me that some people might want to just keep their hobbies as hobbies and enjoy a nice steady income. So how've you been otherwise?"

"Good. I'm dating Dennis Clay. I don't know if you knew that?" She sort of winced as she glanced at me.

"Dennis, huh?" I'd interviewed him during Julie Lewis's murder investigation. He was an attractive guy, seemed nice enough. But...

"I know about what happened in college. He explained it to me. And, I actually called the woman up who'd filed the restraining order. Talked to her about it for a long while. I can see why what he did scared her, but even she agreed now looking back on it that it was probably mostly just different interpretations."

"Hm."

I do believe in listening to women when they come forward with their stories. And filing a restraining order is some serious business. It's more than "Hey, there was a rumor about this guy."

A Puzzling Pooch and Pumpkin Puffs

But I had also had a situation at my job in college where I would've sworn that some dude I worked with was stalking me because he followed me everywhere. I found out years later that yes, he had been following me around the store, I was not wrong about that, but it wasn't because he was interested in me. It was because his sister the manager thought I was stealing. (I wasn't, obviously.)

Regardless of why he was doing it, it made me ill to go into work with him and deal with that for eight hours a day. Eventually I said something not so nice about him in a very public way and got fired.

The feelings I had about that situation definitely existed and were real. But at the same time I was wrong about what had happened.

So...

If that woman had talked to Elaine and had a similar epiphany, I guess I was willing to give Dennis the benefit of the doubt. I guess. But.

I held Elaine's gaze. "Okay. I will trust that you know what you're doing on this. But if he gives you any trouble, any trouble at all, call me and I'll put Matt or my grandpa on it. I don't need to tell you that a man should never hit you or call you nasty names? Ever. Walk if that happens. Okay?"

"Okay. He doesn't though, I promise."

"He also shouldn't follow you around or check up on your movements."

"And he doesn't. It's fine, Maggie. It is."

"If you say so." I gave her one more long look. She seemed fine. So. "I'm glad you're happy and doing well. I'd offer you food or drink or something, but..." I gestured towards our masks. "I'm trying to keep it safe here."

"Understood. And, just so you know, I didn't randomly drop by to chat, I actually had a reason to come by. First, here are some new masks for you guys to wear. Jamie wanted me to bring them by."

(This was back when cloth masks were still the accepted thing. Ah, the good old days...)

I spread out the masks. They were great.

"Look at this one. It has little dancing Newfies on it!"

"I thought you'd like that one. I did a whole bunch with different dog and cat breeds on them for the resort to sell."

"Do you think we'll still need them this summer when we open? I thought things were turning the corner."

Elaine shrugged. "Mason's hedging his bets. All I care about is they're bought and paid for."

"Fair enough. If you're getting paid for them, that's what matters. These are great, Elaine. Thank you so much."

"You're welcome. But that's not actually all of it. I'll be right back." She ran out to her car and came back with a beautiful quilt with turquoise and white panels. When she unfolded it, there were actually two smaller matching quilts. "Jamie said you like blues and turquoises?"

"I do. Oh my gosh. Are these for me? Elaine, they're stunning. These are heirloom pieces."

She beamed at me. "I'm glad you like them. See, by keeping my sewing a hobby I had the time to make them for your girls."

I ran my hand over the panels. They were exquisite. The level of detail work was amazing.

"Elaine..."

A Puzzling Pooch and Pumpkin Puffs

She held up a hand. "You saved my life. And more than that, you're a friend. I wanted to do this for you. The quilts are for when the girls are a little bigger, after they're past the sleeping with no covers to avoid SIDS stage. Once they have their first real beds."

I nodded. "I...I don't know what to say. Thank you. We will treasure these forever."

She smiled. "You're welcome. I'm glad you like them. I better get going. We've got some month-end entries that aren't going to do themselves. But I hope to see you again after the babies are born?"

"Absolutely. We'll figure something out. Thank you again."

I walked her to the door and then went back to stare at the quilts. I was so lucky to have found all these people who made my life that little bit better.

I of course then needed to have a bit of a cry, because pregnancy, hormones, and all that jazz. But once I sniffled my way back into shape it was time to turn my attention to finding Spots' owners once more.

CHAPTER 20

My next call was to the dog shelter down in Denver. The lady on the other end of the line was incredibly nice but absolutely refused to give me the contact information for whoever had adopted Spots.

"But I've seen their dog now. Twice. Don't you think they want him back?" I said.

"Ma'am, I don't know you from Jesus. You could be lying to me right now. You could be telling me you've seen this poor lost dog up in the mountains when what you really are is a stalker trying to get the contact information of some pretty young lady you saw in the park."

"I'm a married woman who's about to give birth to twins. I assure you I have no time for stalking anyone. I just want to return this dog to whoever adopted it from your shelter."

"So you say. Maybe some strange man hired you to call on his behalf to lower my suspicions. I don't know."

I counted to five, slowly. "Look. I am as suspicious as the next girl, so I appreciate your fervent protection of the owner's information. Any woman who has been harassed by some overly-involved weirdo would appreciate what you're doing here. But I would also like to reunite this dog with its owner. So can I maybe instead leave my contact information and ask that you pass it along to whoever adopted the dog?"

"I'm sorry ma'am, but no. For all I know you kidnapped the dog in the first place and this is an elaborate ruse to lure the individual who adopted this dog into meeting you in a remote, lonely location."

"Lady. Either you watch too many true crime shows, read too many crime books, or need some better medication to control the voices. I don't know which it is, but this is absurd. You really won't have them contact me?"

"No. I won't. And if you'll excuse me I have things to do." She hung up.

(Yes, I know the dig about her medication was not nice. I am a work in progress and I was pregnant, tired, and worried about that poor dog, so I was not at my best. People are human, you know, which means not perfect.)

That woman, though, I mean, come on. She was a bit much.

I shook my head. I spent most of my adult life living alone as a single woman. I get it that there are weird men out there.

(My least favorite being the guy who sits close to you on public transport and then proceeds to make a lot of loud noises and move around in a ploy to get you to look at him, so he can then start talking to you because you guys made casual eye contact. See also, the reason someone could literally be choking to death next to me and I'd never once look at them.)

So I get it. But that woman…She took it to a whole new level. She needed to be a writer with an imagination like that.

It left me with a dilemma, though. If I did manage to find the dog, how was I going to get it back to its original owners? Maybe it was microchipped. That would help. Or maybe I could just drop it off at the shelter. Would she find that suspicious?

Since I still didn't know where the dog had been lost or where the owner lived I decided to call all of the animal control offices within a hundred miles of the Baker Valley and of Denver.

Nothing. None had received a report of a missing dog named Spots or one that fit the description I gave.

At that point I was so tired I laid down for another nap.

What? I was pregnant with twins. Give me a break.

CHAPTER 21

I woke up to find a note from my grandpa on the kitchen table. It said he'd dropped by but I'd been sleeping so sound he didn't try to wake me. Instead he'd taken Fancy for a walk (bless the man) and also left a few more containers of food to try from the resort restaurants courtesy of Jamie.

The food looked delicious but I had heartburn that felt like it was going to turn my esophagus into ash, so I settled for much more boring food for my afternoon snack.

The day was warm enough I took Fancy outside and sat on the back porch with her. I only needed a scarf and coat, not the big blanket from the couch. But after twenty minutes I started to shiver a bit and went back in. Fancy stayed out.

I wondered what else there was to do to find Spots. I really couldn't do much until he came back around. I was at a dead-end with the animal control and shelter.

I called Mason and asked him about the house they'd bought as part of the resort development. He was able to point me to his contracts guy who looked the information up for me and confirm that the house Spots had lived at before all of this was only about a quarter mile from where the cabin was located.

"It's still standing if you want to see it," he said. "That section is part of Phase II development. I think they're going to put some horse stables out there."

"We're going to let people bring their horses on vacation?" I asked, mildly appalled.

"I don't know. That's above my pay grade. Might just have horseback riding. But that's not going to happen until next summer according to the development plans."

"Can you tell me exactly where the house is located?"

He rattled off an address and how I could walk there as well as the roads that would get me there. According to his guesstimate, the house was probably only about two-tenths of a mile from where we were if you walked.

"Thank you," I told him and hung up.

Now, knowing me, you are probably thinking to yourself, *"Please tell me she did not try to walk there, end up in labor, and give birth to twins in an abandoned house where she didn't have cellphone service."*

And, granted, that is a valid concern to have, given certain of my past decisions. But I am happy to say that I was a mature, married, mother-to-be who actually took into account the fact that it was not just my personal safety on the line, but the lives of my two little girls as well.

I won't tell you I didn't think about it. Because that would be a lie. But in my defense I did not think about it for long.

Mostly because Matt came home.

And also, my feet were killing me and walking even two-tenths of a mile with ankles as swollen as mine seemed some fresh hell I just could not imagine inflicting upon myself.

So as I lay on the couch with my feet propped up as best I could while dealing with my very large, awkward, uncomfortable belly I instead filled Matt in on everything I'd found out and suggested that maybe we could take a little bit of a drive later?

"It's going to be dark soon, Maggie."

"I know. But...Spots. Another night out there alone without his owner. Struggling to survive in the snow and the cold. Not understanding why he's been abandoned..." I gave him my best hopeful look, but he shook his head.

"Tell ya what. We'll go in the morning. I don't have to be to work until ten and you are always up by six. That should give us plenty of time to drive over there, see if the dog is there, and drive back before I have to leave."

"Thank you. I'd kiss you if I wasn't actually too comfortable to move right this minute."

Of course, the babies being the babies, one of them chose that moment to make me decidedly uncomfortable. I still didn't kiss Matt, though. I was too busy trying to get to the bathroom in time.

Ah, the joys of pregnancy.

CHAPTER 22

Matt and I drove over to the address I'd been given the next morning. It was weird having to put on real clothes. I'd gotten away with hanging out in really soft baggy pajamas since we'd moved to the cabin because the only people who were going to see me were basically family.

Well, and Mason, but who cares about impressing Mason? I was pretty sure he already had his opinions of me and my wearing comfortable pajamas for a lunchtime meeting weren't going to change them.

Greta, too, I guess, but she has a way of not seeing what she doesn't want to see, so if she was offended I never noticed.

The house was down a dirt road that had clearly not been plowed or leveled recently. We were fortunate that Matt's police vehicle was built for pretty much any terrain.

And that it had good shocks. Even with good shocks it was a bumpy drive. After the third time I put my hand against my belly and said, "Oof", Matt suggested that maybe we should turn back.

But no way no how was I giving up on my one chance

to check out the house and find Spots.

We'd had a decent run of good weather for Colorado in winter, but we were due for snow that night and I did not want him out in it. (Sometimes in Colorado the forecast and the actual timing of the snow don't exactly match, but they're usually within a day or two and a foot or two of one another.)

Finally, when I was really starting to question the woman who'd lived there's sanity for living in the absolute Boondocks, we turned a corner and saw the place.

I understood in that moment why she'd lived there. It was so peaceful. And the house was so cute. It was one story with a fenced-in yard and trees all around. Not too close—fire danger and all—but close enough to make it feel cozy.

I loved it. I could see why Spots had come back to it, too. It was perfect.

(Okay, so maybe I was anthropomorphizing the dog a bit, his feelings were probably not complex human emotions, he just wanted to get back to his person and his home. But I did really love the place and could see why someone would want to live there even if it was in the butt end of nowhere.)

You know, I think it's a travesty for people who've grown up somewhere like New York City or downtown DC to not at least be given a chance to experience nature like that.

Get them away from the concrete and tall buildings, and the people everywhere and the non-stop noise, and the lights and stress, and let them see what else the world can be. Take them somewhere where they can only hear birds chirping in the distance or wind blowing through the trees.

Yes, I know, some people would shudder at the thought of so much loneliness and silence. But in my opinion there is almost no manmade beauty that can trump nature.

Although mankind does come close sometimes. I'm not particularly religious but I still think of a stone carving I saw of Jesus once in an old church in Avila, Spain. Took my breath away.

And if you've ever watched the Keira Knightley version of *Pride and Prejudice* there's a carving in there when she's walking through Darcy's house that gets me every time. Like how did they do that? That stone carving of a woman with a veil? Remarkable.

But nature. Nature is epic on a scale that a tall building can never touch. At least for me.

We pulled up in front of the house and I glanced at Matt. "What do you think of the house?"

We'd tried looking for homes in the valley, but there were barely any listings. And almost all of them had multiple stories which I was not going to do unless it was the house I already hated that was next door to my grandpa and was at least saved by virtue of its location. The other houses in our price range—which was not a high-priced range—were rundown sorts of places missing key features like running water and electricity.

So that house…Even with its dirt road…Looked like perfection.

"What do you mean?" Matt asked. "What about it?"

"Well, we haven't found a place to live yet. I mean, we can stay next to Grandpa, but that place has stairs and with two small kids and two dogs…"

"*Two* dogs?"

"Uh, sorry. One dog."

He narrowed his eyes at me. "You don't make that kind of mistake, Maggie."

I held up a hand. "Look, I don't know what'll happen here. But if we find the dog and we can't find the owners, maybe instead of sending it back to the pound…"

"Right." He gave me a look.

"Just think about it. And I'll see what the situation with this house is. If it's available, would you want to live here?"

"Just like that? You haven't even been inside. It could be falling down, rat-infested, stink like cat urine…"

"But it's perfect. Especially if we're both going to be working for the resort. It's close enough to be on call, but far enough to be private. And one story. You know how much I hate stairs. I mean, I assume it's one story. It could have a basement I guess. In which case, that's yours. Do you like doing laundry?"

He didn't dignify my question with an answer, but instead studied the house and the area around us. "I do like it. If the inside matches the outside, it has some potential. We'd need to get that road paved, though. Or at least planed and some potholes filled in."

"Ha. Yes! I knew it."

"But only if the inside looks doable. We're too close to your due date for massive renovations. Whatever it looks like inside, we're going to have to go with."

"But otherwise?" I stared at him hopefully. "Let me remind you how much I love you."

"Because I go along with everything you want?"

"Because you go along with *almost* everything I want but push back when I take it too far. So?"

"Let's find out more and then we can decide. But for now…A tentative yes."

I bounced in my seat. Which really made me want to pee, but that was just going to have to not happen. "Great. Let's find the dog."

We stepped out of the vehicle and I took a deep breath of the crisp winter air. It even smelled good.

"Spots," I called. "Come here boy. Come here, Spots."

"I'll go look around back," Matt said.

"Okay."

As he disappeared around the side of the house, I hustled up to the porch and peeked in the window by the front door. It was…not rat-infested.

I could see a cute little kitchen. It had those old brown wood cabinets from back in the day—that would need to be painted over at some point—but at least there were actual cabinets. *And* no granite countertops or stainless steel appliances. Yay.

(I know. People love those things. But did you know that you have to reseal granite countertops? And that you have to be careful not to get acidic things—like lemon juice—on them or they'll stain? And the last stainless steel fridge I'd had wouldn't take a fridge magnet either. Now, granted my putting twenty fridge magnets from all the places I've traveled on a fridge should probably be strongly discouraged, but to not even be able to put a memo pad up? And I was about to have kids. I needed somewhere for their artwork.)

The other window showed a living room with wood

paneling and some unfortunate carpet. I winced at that. I actually like carpet, but not shag orange carpet. And it did make me worry about potential smells.

But it could all be dealt with. The structure seemed sound at least. I didn't see dirt or pine needles on the floor. And, really, what other choice did we have at that point? We had tried, trust me. The location was perfect and that's what really counted. All the rest could be fixed.

Even if it did take us ten years to do it, because, you know, twins. I winced again. Orange shag carpet for a decade?

Not ideal. But it was what it was. I turned my attention back to calling for Spots, but he never appeared.

Matt did, about five minutes later. "I found an old dog house in the backyard. It was in pretty rough shape but I scavenged some loose boards and patched it up as best I could. I'm going to put that blanket we brought and the water bowl out, just in case.

"Good idea. We can come back in a few days and see if maybe it's being used."

He chuckled. "Probably find a fox or raccoon or something when we do."

"Well, if there is we'll still have done a good deed. All God's creatures and what not. As long as it's not a skunk family. Not that they don't also deserve shelter, just, you know, I'd rather you didn't come home smelling like skunk."

"Agreed."

As he went back to put the blanket and water bowl in place I shook a bag of treats and called for Spots one more time, but still nothing. Either he wasn't there or he was so scared he wouldn't come out.

I really hoped we'd find him before the next big snowstorm. Poor guy. But at that point we'd pretty much done what we could. If he wanted to be found he was going to have to come to us.

CHAPTER 23

When we returned to the cabin, Matt left for work and I took a couple-hour nap until my meeting with Jamie. She came in with Max in his carrier and a big smile on her face.

"Good morning," she almost sang.

"You seem happy."

"I am. Look what just arrived. Aren't they gorgeous?"

She held up one of those "We Believe" signs. You know the signs I'm talking about? They're all pretty and cute and start with "In this house we believe" and then list things like "love is love" and "kindness is everything" and all that?

"Uh. Nice. For your front yard?"

"No. For here. I thought we could put them in the windows of all the cabins."

I pressed my lips together.

Jamie stared at me in horror. I think it was the first time I'd ever seen her worry that something was fundamentally wrong with me.

(Which, given my history, says a lot.)

"You don't support these signs? You don't believe that

black lives matter and science is real and no human is illegal? Maggie, I…I don't know what to say."

I put my hands together and pressed them to my lips. I knew Jamie meant well, but…

I sighed and laced my fingers together.

"Okay. Sorry, but you're about to get a rant you probably didn't want to hear." I opened my mouth to continue but had to pause to figure out how to put into words what I wanted to say. "First, I think having a sign like that in your yard is good, right? Because it's a public statement of some very important beliefs that I think are good beliefs to have. And publicly stating these things matters. It lets others know they're not alone in believing these things and maybe makes people who don't believe these things pause for a moment and reconsider. Maybe."

"But?" She stared at me like a wide-eyed doe seeing a hunter about to shoot its mom.

"But…" I took a deep breath. "I think for the most part those signs are performative bullshit used by upper middle class white people to pretend they care."

As she stared at me like I'd just shot her, I continued my rant. Might as well. I'd gone too far at that point to stop. "I mean, really, Black Lives Matter is in bright pink and No Human Is Illegal is in a pretty shade of blue. I get that people want a lawn sign that's attractive, but come on. Not to mention, probably eighty percent of the people who put a sign like that in their window or their yard are then going to turn around and explain to you how their husband absolutely deserves to earn three hundred thousand a year for all his hard work while his company won't even hire a black person for a similar role because 'it wasn't a good cultural fit' which is just privilege-speak for doesn't sound and look like me."

I barely paused for breath as I added, "And ask one of those people to vote on something that might infringe their perfect life to help black people or immigrants or anyone else captured by that sign and they're going to vote it down in a second. Because as much as they're willing to put a pretty sign up and sound outraged about the world today they're not willing to actually give up something *they* have to make things better."

I shrugged and turned towards the kitchen. "Sorry. It's just a pet peeve of mine. Too much time on Twitter where people talk about their outrage instead of logging off and actually sitting down with frustrating people to try to create real, impactful change."

As I made a cup of tea, I added, "At least you didn't bring in a blue line flag. Nothing like desecrating the symbol of your own country to show your support for the police. Frickin' idiots."

There was absolute silence until I returned to the table. Jamie looked at the sign in front of her and then back at me, stricken. I wanted to apologize for what I'd said, but it was true. At least in my opinion.

(Of course, not saying I'm any better. I try to vote for the collective good which is why even before I had kids I voted for school funding and libraries and things like that. But I'm just as prone to sit on my butt as the next person and just as prone to complain without taking action. I just happen to also complain about the people who complain is all. Ah, irony, my good friend.)

I squeezed Jamie's hand. "Ignore me. Please. I'm pregnant and cranky and full of weird ideas. All I ask is

if you are going to put those up around the property—
and you may want to check with your husband first
since, you know, he may vote differently than you
think—is that you also remember all those pithy sayings
du jour next time you go to vote and that you try to live
them. And that if we as a corporate entity donate
money, that we do so to politicians or causes that
actually support what those signs say and not to the
assholes who'll lower our corporate taxes while going
against everything listed there."

I hated to upset my friend, especially when I knew she
meant well and believed in what was on those signs. But
there'd been a time in my life when I tried not to talk
politics or religion with anyone ever and look where that
got us.

"So," I said. "How's Max doing? He looks great, as
always."

Her shoulders sagged in relief. Jamie is the most
competent person I know, but conflict is not something
she enjoys.

"He's been fidgety this week. I think it's probably just
growing pains. But I'm keeping an eye on it. After I took
him into the doctor four times in the first four weeks I try
to let things work themselves out before I involve her.
But it's hard."

I laughed. "I can imagine. Did I ever tell you about
the time I took Fancy into the vet because I thought
she'd cracked a tooth?"

"No. What happened?"

"She lost one of her back baby teeth but it looked so
completely different from her front teeth that I assumed
she'd cracked a tooth and rushed her to the vet. He was

so embarrassed on my behalf he told me to sneak out the back door and pretend I'd never been there. At least he didn't bill me for it."

"What a nice vet."

"He was. One of my big regrets about moving was losing that vet and gaining Mr. Crankypants Your Dog Is Fat as a replacement."

"He said that about Lulu, too!"

We talked dogs and babies for the next half hour. I was glad we'd been able to find our way back to a middle ground where we could joke and laugh. I hadn't meant to single her out about the sign thing, it was just something that really irked me, this modern trend of trying to boil serious issues down to slogans and signage.

It made me worry for my girls, what our world was becoming.

(I know these stories I tell you are supposed to be light and fluffy and fun and an escape for both of us, but the world is right there, you know, and I can't help but being shaped by it, and sometimes that leaks through. Sorry. Not sorry. But sorry.)

Anyway. I digress.

Jamie and I had a good visit in the end. She promised to look into that house for me and see if we could live in it, which was good progress, but I still hadn't found Spots and my delivery date was coming closer every single day that passed.

CHAPTER 24

The next week was uneventful.

Given the number of times Fancy went racing outside barking her head off either Spots was lurking nearby or a mountain lion was. Or maybe both.

My stomach continued to get bigger—something I really hadn't thought was possible—and my back pretty much ached non-stop all day no matter what position I was in.

To cheer me up the doctor did one of those creepy 3D ultrasounds. Have you ever seen one of those things? The babies look like aliens because they're in this reddish-copper color that is not the color of human skin. At all. And they're not quite done developing just yet, so it's even more freaky.

It's just not right. Give me the blurry black and white images of the old days anytime, because the last thing I needed as I approached the end of my pregnancy was something that made me wonder exactly what was growing inside me.

I'd also taken to listening to music all the time to keep the babies entertained. I'd like to tell you I listened to calming, beautiful classical music that would elevate their tastes, but that would be a lie.

I figured if my girls were going to have to grow up on classical rock like Cream and Blood, Sweat, & Tears they might as well get used to it now. That and Taylor Swift, P!nk, Jim Croce, and Kenny Rogers.

What can I say? I'm eclectic. (Right, that's the word for it. Eclectic. Better than describing me as someone with as many personalities as there are sides on a thirty-sided die.)

Even though most of my research had indicated that bed rest was not the best idea in the world for most women, I did end up getting a lot of rest simply because I was tired.

The day I made it to 36 weeks I wanted to get up and dance around the room, but I settled for a "hell yeah" as I walked to the kitchen for another glass of tea.

That's when Spots made his next appearance. Fancy was in the living room sleeping when I saw him out in the yard. Quietly I blocked the doggie door, grabbed a bag of treats, put on my coat and warm slippers, and went outside.

The treats woke Fancy up, of course, but I was able to throw her a few and sneak out the door before she tried to follow.

"Hey, Spots," I said in my friendliest dog voice. "How are you, buddy?"

His little tail wagged.

"Do you want a treat?" I tossed one of the treats near him. He flinched when it hit the ground but then approached it cautiously, sniffed it for a few seconds, and gobbled it up.

I kept throwing him treats, each one closer to me than the last, until he was on the porch next to me. He was in rough shape. The scratch on his nose did not look good at all. He was also limping on one foot. And there were more than just pine needles tangled in his coat. On his hip he had a whole branch tangled up in his hair.

"Ah, you poor thing." I wanted to pet him, but he was still pretty skittish. Also, fleas and dirt and what-have-you.

"Hm. What to do with you now?"

The porch had a gate you could pull shut so that it was closed in. The railing was slatted and only hip-height, but with Fancy that would've been more than enough to keep her contained. I figured I could shut him in on the porch and then call Jamie or Matt or my grandpa to come help.

I slowly eased around behind him and pulled the gate shut as he ate another treat.

But that's when I learned that the little guy was quite the escape artist. The railing on the patio was about three feet high maybe? He jumped right over it.

From a standing position.

No running leap like I would've needed (and still failed). Nope, just a quick, pop! right over the railing.

He took off for the woods as I called after him to come back and never even hesitated for a moment as he reached the bigger fence and jumped right over that one, too. At least that let me know how he'd been getting into the yard since I never had found a loose board or hole.

He was gone in a moment.

I let Fancy out into the yard and she raced over every inch of it, her nose pressed to the ground, pausing to pee occasionally, presumably where he'd tried to mark his territory.

Great.

I'd missed him again and all I had to show for it was a very sulky, very big dog who ignored me for the rest of the afternoon. Joy.

CHAPTER 25

Jamie came over about twenty minutes later.

"Any word on that house?" I asked. "Do you think Matt and I could rent it? I wish we could buy it, but since it's part of the resort I know that's not an option…"

I was still nervous about renting a house from the resort. I mean, what if it failed? Matt and I would both lose our jobs, *and* we'd lose our home all in one big fell swoop.

But I put that aside because that kind of paranoid catastrophizing is just what I call a normal Tuesday.

Jamie wouldn't meet my eyes. "Um, you know, still looking into it."

I knew I should let it go, but I was worried. Time was running short. And if we couldn't have the house to rent then I needed to know. I wondered if my asking had been some sort of unspoken breach of etiquette. Sometimes I miss class differences and maybe Mason had been offended by the idea we'd rent from the resort and Jamie just didn't want to tell me.

See, this is why you don't involve family and friends in money or business. Because it gets awkward.

I rubbed at my back. I could not get comfortable anymore. "Jamie, please be honest with me. If we can't have the place, just say so." I winced as the muscles in my belly tightened.

"Are you okay?" she asked.

"Fine. Just the normal aches and pains of being a living, breathing incubator. I can't believe that one woman had eight babies at once. Like, how?"

"Well, they're really small when that happens. She probably had an easier birth than a woman who has one really big baby."

"Right. That makes sense. Miserable pregnancy, easier birth. If all you had to do was carry and give birth to the kids then multiples would be the best choice. But then you also have to raise them…Can you imagine? Eight kids at once? As a single mom."

"I know. Crazy, right?"

"Me, I'm just in the sad middle ground where I get both a miserable pregnancy and a hard birth." I winced again.

"Maggie?"

"It's fine. When you get this big, it hurts. And I'm just a little stressed is all. You sure you don't have news on the house? It would really help to know. One way or the other."

She shook her head. "Sorry. You know Mason and business and all that…"

I tried to hide my disappointment. Where were going to live? I guess we could always go back to the place by my grandpa. It wasn't *bad*. And maybe we could move in a couple years? Although, moving with toddlers? Ugh.

I frowned. I knew we were going to be stuck in that place for the next decade. And…I didn't want to be. But nothing to do about it. If I'd crossed some horrible invisible line with Mason I'd just have to hope it didn't impact anything else. See, this is why you didn't work with friends and family.

Work-only relationships were so much cleaner.

Although, no, not really. I'd always been stepping in it when I had a corporate job. I mean, seriously, casually mention that your grandpa had spent fifteen years in prison and suddenly everyone is like, "Oh, you're not one of us."

Well, at least they are after they find out it was for armed robbery and not some white-collared version of stealing from people. A little Ponzi scheme is just a misstep between friends. But armed robbery? That's simply not done. If you're wealthy you don't use *guns* to take people's money. How crass and obvious.

I sighed deeply.

Jamie squeezed my arm. "It'll work out. Trust me."

"Heh. Yeah. Right. It'll work out. Of course it will."

Luckily for Jamie, because I think it was starting to get awkward at that point, the babies decided that was the perfect time to arrive.

What had been sort of consistent but widely-spaced pains in my stomach suddenly started to get a lot more regular and a lot more frequent.

I stared up at her. "Oh God. I think it's time. You need to take me to the hospital."

"It's time? For the babies?"

I nodded. "Yep."

"I'll call Matt."

"Do that. But tell him to meet us at the hospital. We need to go. Now."

"Now?"

I nodded my head vigorously as another contraction came. "Yep. Now. Right now. Let's go. Now."

"Maggie…"

"You know those pains I'd been feeling the last day or so? Pretty sure those were labor. So, yeah, now. Right now."

CHAPTER 26

One of the reasons Jamie is my best friend is because there is almost no occasion she can't handle. So when I told her "now", she took control. She had me and my go bag bundled into the back of her vehicle within five minutes and had called Matt and my grandpa by the time we pulled out of the cabin's driveway.

As we drove to the hospital at a slightly-above-speed-limit-but-not-dangerously-fast speed she called Mason and asked him to drop in and grab Fancy.

I wanted to object—I mean, Mason?—but she was right. Who else would she call? I wanted my husband and my grandpa at the hospital and at least Fancy knew Mason and would tolerate him well enough.

The folks at the hospital knew about me and fortunately didn't drag their feet when we showed up. Which, as it turns out, was a very good thing. Because despite my mom's stories of being in labor with me for like twenty-four-plus hours, I was in labor at the hospital for a grand total of thirty-five minutes.

The doctors were not happy with me for waiting so long and thought I'd done it deliberately, but I swear, I had not. I just couldn't tell the difference between "this is labor" and "this is the unending miserable, cramping existence that you have been condemned to until you give birth" that had been my last week or so of pregnancy.

They made me deliver in an operating room since there was a chance that even if I got baby one out just fine that baby two would need to come out via C-section. Doctors take a woman giving birth to twins seriously. Which, I should be glad for, but it's a little stressful, you know?

Like, *Here, we've got this whole surgical tray set up right there by your side so we can cut into you and grab that baby out if we need to at any moment. Ready to push?* Cue fake smile.

Oh, and just because it was a short labor does not mean it was a painless labor. No epidural for me. And things…yeah. Let's just not go there, huh?

At least the twins were on the smaller side, which made it easier. But not too small, thankfully. They squeaked in just under the line.

I was almost nine pounds when I was born (ouch), but my little girls weighed in at 5.5 lbs each. And by some miracle they were both fine to breathe on their own, too. And both had ten fingers and ten toes and everything else in the right place. No hair, though. They were as bald as I'd been when I was born.

Baby one had some seriously good lungs. Holy cow. She came into the world letting everybody know exactly what she thought of being removed from her very comfortable home.

Baby number two came out wide-eyed and calm and looking around like she already knew more than all of us combined.

(Which, well, that's pretty much how my girls have gone through the world since. Baby one leading with a screaming charge, baby two coming along behind and not missing a thing.)

And, yeah, in that moment I felt what everyone says you feel. That as covered in who-knows-what and as screaming as baby one was and as much as it had hurt and I'd ached and suffered to get to that moment, that it was worth it to hold those little girls in my arms and know that they were mine in a way that nothing in this world had ever been before.

I expected they weren't going to appreciate me as a mom when they were stubborn-minded independent teenagers, but even then they'd still be a part of me. And a part of Matt.

Hopefully they'd be the best of the both of us combined and two unique, amazing individuals at the same time.

It was amazing.

And also the beginning of one of the scariest, most rewarding journeys of my life. Heck, it was even scarier than jumping out of a plane.

Fortunately, I was so exhausted after weeks of not getting enough sleep that even the thought of what was ahead couldn't keep me awake for more than the time it took to have everyone tell me how happy they were for me.

CHAPTER 27

I woke up sometime that night to find Matt sitting in a chair by my bed, wide awake.

"Hey, did you get some sleep?" I asked, rubbing at my eyes.

He shook his head. "No. I've been sitting here watching over you and the girls. Your superstitiousness must've rubbed off. I had this crazy thought that if I closed my eyes, it would all go away. This was the most amazing day of my life and I didn't want it to end."

I reached out and he laced his fingers through mine.

"We did pretty good, you know," I said.

"We did. Now can we name them, though?"

I laughed softly as I rested my head against the pillow. "Right. They can't just be our bundles of joy anymore. They need real live names."

"We could name one Joy, so they still are in a sense." He raised an eyebrow, looking at me expectantly.

I nodded. "We could..."

I'd gone to school with a girl named Muffie whose parents had given her that name because they'd told her older brother there was a muffin in the oven for the entire pregnancy, and they figured that would help him understand that the little baby they brought home was the same as that muffin in the oven.

Poor girl. Stuck with an unfortunate name like that for her entire life just so her brother would be able to connect the two. (In some weird way the name actually fit even though she was not an east coast prep school student or bubbly cheerleader. I guess that's what happens when you have such a unique name. You can make it your own.)

Anyway. I was still in post-delivery, pregnancy delirium, so I added, "And, maybe, I mean, right now, things seem to finally be turning the corner in the world after a dark stretch, so maybe the other one could be Hope? Hope and Joy?"

(I know. How cheesy can you get? But I'd just given birth. There was blood loss involved. Do you think my mind was working in a rational way? I think there are some cultures that wait something like forty-five days to give newborns names. Those people are smart. Because, well...)

Matt smiled. "I like that. Hope and Joy."

(I don't know what Matt's excuse was. He was supposed to be the one that stopped me from making bad life decisions, not enabled them. But, maybe he was tired, too.)

I glanced over to where the babies were starting to stir. "They're going to hate us for it, you know that, right? And it pretty much guarantees that at least one of them is going to be a bitter and jaded goth princess when she's a teenager who sneaks out of the house, smokes, drinks, and tells us she hates us all the time."

He laughed. "If her entry into the world is any indication, I'm pretty sure baby number one is going to be that way no matter what name we give her."

"True. Less than twenty-four hours in and we're already in trouble. Hm. Maybe Joy isn't such a great choice for her." I chuckled.

"We could name them after your mom and your grandma."

I shook my head. "We could. But I want them to be their own people, you know? Not burdened by some legacy of an earlier generation. Also Olivia, Emma, Ava, Charlotte, and Sophia are out, too."

"Why?"

"Most common baby names last year. I always pitied the Sarahs and Jennifers in my class who had to be Sarah B or Jenny J so you could tell them apart from the other Sarahs and Jennifers. I was always the only Maggie, you know, which was nice."

"Hm."

I realized he'd probably been a Matt B himself. Maybe it wasn't so bad being on that end of things after all.

We sat there for a long moment, thinking about our choices.

"So Hope and Joy?" Matt finally asked.

"You realize we're bringing on the apocalypse if we name them that? The world is just going to go to shit if we do this. That means we also need a good solid middle name they might actually want to use, unlike May for me. My mom used to tell me I could use my middle name if I didn't like my first name, but May just never had any flavor to it, you know."

(No offense, of course, to anyone named May. But when you move from Maggie to May there's a shift there. People do react to names and the way they view a Maggie is not the way they view a May. Sorry to say it.)

"What are you thinking?" he asked.

"I don't know. I kind of want to give them both the same middle name, but we can't do that. Can we?"

"Why not?"

"What if they *both* hate their names? And then they both want to go by their middle name? Twins with the same name? How awful would that be."

He shrugged. "If they do, they do. I know you're going to dress them alike. You won't be able to resist."

"Only for birthdays and holidays, I swear. When we can really have fun with it and take lots of photos. The rest of the time they can do whatever they want. Maybe they'll each get a signature color, you know. For years when I was a kid it seemed like everything I was given was lilac."

"And did you like that?"

"No."

"Well, then maybe we skip the colors. At least until they're old enough to choose them themselves."

We lapsed back into silence.

Matt squeezed my hand. "So. What middle name can we choose that will work for both of them?"

"What about Rosenda? It's a family middle name on my side if you go back a few generations, but no one ever used it as their main name. And there's a lot of variations they could use so they could be the same but different."

He nodded. "I like it. So baby one is Joy Rosenda Barnes-Carver and baby two is Hope Rosenda Barnes-Carver."

I squeezed his hand. "Just Barnes, no need to hyphenate."

"Does that mean you changed your mind about taking my last name?"

"Nope. But I also don't think our babies need hyphenated last names either. Imagine learning how to write that. Ugh. Hey, that's another reason Hope and Joy are good choices. They're short. Ooh, and Barnes, too. Lucky kids."

He smiled. "Okay, then. Joy Rosenda Barnes and Hope Rosenda Barnes who will likely end up calling themselves Roz and Rosie by the time they're eighteen."

I laughed. "Perfect."

Our eyes met and I shivered. "I can't believe we're doing this. I'm glad I have you by my side. I don't think I could do it alone."

He kissed my forehead. "You could. And you would. But I'm glad I'm here, too. There is nowhere I'd rather be than with my girls."

(Yes, it was hokey. Optimism, exhaustion, and lack of sleep do that to you. And, yes, we probably did bring on ten years of bad luck with those names. But it was a really good moment. Of course, I still hadn't found Spots yet and we still didn't have anywhere to live permanently…but life is messy like that sometimes. And you gotta take the wins when they come.)

CHAPTER 28

Two days after I gave birth, we headed "home" with the twins.

Of course, home was still the cabin at the resort, because we still had no idea where we were going to live. At least I didn't. Matt had promised me that he had something in the works, but he wouldn't tell me what. I figured it was some sort of renovation on the house next to my grandpa's or maybe we were swapping out with Jack and Trish and we'd live in Matt's dad's old mobile home and they'd live next to my grandpa.

I didn't really mind the thought of living there. The views were gorgeous. And, sure, yeah, it was a mobile home not a home home, but really when you're in one it doesn't feel any different. It's more the tornado risks and freezing pipes and predatory landlords that are the issue with a mobile home. But if we owned the property and were well-insulated…

It wasn't a bad option. It wasn't the house on the resort property, but, you know, you don't always get what you want. Sometimes you just have to find a solution that at least gives you what you need. (Thanks,

Rolling Stones, for that life lesson.)

I was so exhausted learning how to nurse and then nursing two babies that I really didn't care at that point. Give me a roof over my head, food, and a safe place to sleep and that was good enough for me.

Poor Fancy was beside herself when we got there. (Matt had already been by earlier in the day to get her settled back into the cabin and to arrange the basics we were going to need, but last she'd seen me I'd rushed out in pain and then she'd had *Mason* show up. I don't know what she had to be thinking at that point.)

I figured she'd be pretty emotional about everything so when we pulled up I left Matt with the babies in the van and went in on my own first. I was actually able to sit on the floor with her for the first time in a couple of months. (Even though that wasn't the best of ideas post delivery, I knew she needed it.)

I let her crawl all over me as she gave me a long lecture and licked at my face frantically.

"It's okay, Fancy. I promise."

She finally settled enough for me to pet her some and give her a kiss on the forehead. I rubbed at her velvety soft ears. "You and me, kiddo. It's going to be a wild ride, but we'll make it work."

When I stood back up and reached for the door she looked at me in panic. "I'll be right back. I promise. I'm coming right back. It's okay." I gently closed the door in her face.

I could've probably let her come out to the van with me, I was pretty sure she wouldn't run away, but you never know, and I did not need to lose her when trying to care for two newborns.

She was right there at the door when Matt and I came back in with a carrier each. I had to nudge her to the side as she tried to sniff at Joy who was just starting to stir from what had been a nice, peaceful nap.

I set the carrier down on the couch. "What do you think, Fancy?"

She sniffed at Joy and then turned to sniff at Hope when Matt set her down, too. After she'd finished her inspection she turned to look at me.

"Do you like them?"

In answer she laid herself down along the length of the couch between the two carriers and closed her eyes with a contented sigh.

"I'd say that's a yes. I bet she's going to be their Nana dog like in the Peter Pan books."

Matt put his arm around my shoulders. "I couldn't think of a better protector for my girls."

As Matt went off to reheat one of the casseroles Lesley had left us and I settled in for (yet another) nursing session with the twins, Fancy stayed right where she was, keeping an eye on me as I nursed Joy and then Hope.

When I moved to the table to eat, she didn't budge, though. Not even when I set down a sharing plate for her. It seemed babies trumped food in Fancyworld. Interesting.

Matt laughed. "I wonder if Fancy will ever leave their sides again."

"She'll have to at some point."

We ate that whole meal without Fancy even looking in our direction once. She only moved when Joy woke up again and started crying for milk. And then all she did was jump to her feet and look at me like, "Alright, do something already. Help my baby out here, would ya?"

I'd been so worried that Fancy would feel left out when we brought the babies home, but honestly I was the one that felt like I'd been abandoned, because from that day forward those little girls were her world.

CHAPTER 29

That afternoon my grandpa and Lesley came by.

"Don't look," my grandpa told me as he had Matt go back out to the truck with him.

Lesley—with her pure white hair in an adorable bob and her tactful pearls—distracted me by showing me all of the meals she'd brought to fill up our freezer.

"Has anyone ever told you you're a lifesaver?" I asked her.

She smiled. "I know what it's like in those first few days. Which is why there are also boxes of snacks in the truck that we'll bring in in a minute just in case the effort of heating something up feels like too much."

Each container was labeled in her perfect-looking script. It was every type of casserole you could possibly want.

"Good thing I have Matt around to be my home helper. He can heat the food while I lounge on the couch being a milk-producing factory."

Lesley laughed and patted my hand. "You'll get used to it eventually."

(I wasn't sure I actually believed that, but I was willing to pretend in the hopes that she was right.)

My grandpa and Matt came back inside muttering to one another as they maneuvered something through the door.

The cradle!

I'd forgotten. In all the excitement and stress and insanity I'd forgotten that my grandpa was making the babies a cradle.

"Don't turn around yet, Maggie May," my grandpa called as he and Matt headed back outside.

"What on earth did he make?" I asked Lesley as they came in and went back outside a third time.

"You'll see. Some of it isn't what he made. We have goodies for you as well."

Finally, my grandpa said, "Okay, Maggie May. Turn around."

I turned. There were *two* wooden cradles sitting in the middle of the living room. They were exquisite. Gorgeous.

Honestly, I can't do them justice.

They smelled like cedar (which is such a good smell) but my grandpa had inlaid different types of wood at each end on the outside to make these gorgeous patterns so that they looked like works of art.

They *were* works of art.

And at the top above where the babies heads would go, each one had an arch with the baby's name carved in cursive in the center with roses around the perimeter.

"How did you find the time to make two of them? And when did you add the names?" I asked as I ran my fingers over the intricate carvings.

He flexed his hand and winced. "Spent the whole day yesterday finishing 'em up. Everything was set except for the names. And the roses. I added those when Matt told us what their middle names were going to be."

"These are so amazing, Grandpa." I started crying.

Matt chuckled and put his arm around my shoulder. "Ignore her. She's been doing that a lot since she got pregnant."

I wiped the tears away. "I hope it stops soon. This crying at everything is getting to be a bit much."

I stepped away from Matt to give my grandpa a big hug. "Thank you so much. These are so special to me." I wiped at my cheeks again. "Sorry."

"Don't worry. It's not a bad thing to cry." He pulled back and looked me in the eyes. "But if you find that you're crying for no reason, then you tell someone. I had a friend whose wife had that post-partum and it was bad. So no going it alone. I know we have to limit our visits to keep you and the babies safe, but I'm going to call you every day and check on you."

I smiled and hugged him again. "Thank you. I'm so glad I have you."

"Oh, and the name plaques at the top of the cradles there? Those can be removed when the babies are done with the cradles. Maybe you can put them on the wall above their beds or on their doors or something."

"That's amazing, Grandpa. You think of everything."

Lesley grabbed my hand and led me to the corner where there were two large plastic bins. "Now, I know you didn't want a baby shower, but people still wanted to buy you cute gifts. So I collected them on your behalf. With twins we didn't know what size they'd be or when they'd arrive, so I did most of the clothes shopping in a rush after you delivered. That'll all arrive tomorrow—

gotta love two-day shipping—but in these bins there are diapers and baby wipes and diaper cream and burp cloths and the rest of it to get you started."

I stared at her, wide-eyed. "To get me started? There's two bins of stuff there."

She laughed. "Oh, you just wait. You'll be amazed at how much stuff you have by the time you hit the six-month mark."

I glanced around the small living room area of the cabin and then at Matt, horror in my eyes.

He came and hugged me. "Deep breaths. We've got this."

"Right. Deep breaths. We've got this."

But did we? All my research online and I honestly did not know what I was doing. Other girls babysat or had younger siblings growing up, but I'd had none of that. And I'd studiously avoided being around babies my whole adult life because I didn't want to break one.

(And you think I'm exaggerating, but I actually had a friend's kid stand on my leg at one point when he was not that old. I was holding him, kind of bouncing him, and then that kid pushed off against my leg and twisted around like a salmon. I almost dropped him on his head on the floor. No way I was going to try to hold another baby after that…)

So my entire baby experience was limited to a few times when I was brave enough to try to hold Max. But Matt had been around when Jack was young, so maybe he had a clue what to do about all of it. Maybe.

Fortunately, Lesley spent the next hour walking me through all the things she'd brought and why I needed them and how to use them, or I would've been completely lost.

There were so many things. And so much to do. I had flashbacks to when Fancy was a puppy and how hard that had been, but Lesley patted my hand. "You'll be fine. Don't worry."

We had a good meal together and then they left.

And that's when it hit me, Matt and I were committed to this path for the next eighteen years. I didn't have time to freak out about it, though, because Joy woke up screaming for food.

"Time to feed 'em, yet again." I collapsed onto the couch as Matt picked her up from her cradle.

Fancy, who had established herself between the two cradles watched Matt carefully to make sure he didn't drop her and then put her head back down on her paws when he'd successfully handed her off to me.

Do you know how hard breastfeeding is? I knew all the reasons to do it, so I was determined to give a good try, but with two babies to feed? Holy…

Not easy. But I did it because that's what you do. And then…

When the babies were settled and changed and back asleep?

I took a nap. The nurses had said I needed lots of rest and that I should get it while the babies were sleeping, so that's exactly what I did, leaving poor Matt and Fancy to entertain themselves.

CHAPTER 30

I hadn't forgotten about Spots. If he was still out there all alone he couldn't be doing well. I mean, snow and wilderness. It had to be rough.

I'd actually once seen a picture of a Newfie who'd gone "wild". Poor thing had a matted coat six inches thick that had to be shaved off when it was finally brought in. I didn't want that to happen to Spots. But, giving birth had sort of derailed my plans to find the poor guy.

Day three of being home I was finally working myself up to having enough energy to drive over there and track him down, but I wasn't quite there yet.

I decided I'd do it after the babies, Matt, and I spent a little time outside. Fancy had been inside with me while I was pregnant and then with them, so I knew she had to be dying to get outside and just lie in some grass for a bit.

I figured after we had our outing maybe Matt could watch the girls for me while I drove over there.

(Yes, the logical option would've been to have Matt drive over, but I was a little stir-crazy, too, by that point.

I needed a reminder that I was more than just a milk-vending and diaper-changing machine.)

At least the weather had finally started to turn towards spring so it was warm enough to sit in the shade and not freeze. Matt and I bundled the girls up, though, just to be safe.

They were in adorable matching coats and pink hats with bear ears. (I hadn't wanted to go the matchy-matchy route, but it seems Lesley or whoever else ordered clothes for them had. I'd given in because how can you resist such adorable cuteness as matching ladybug outfits? I'd also had to give in on the pink and sparkly thing or else the kids wouldn't have had much to wear.)

As soon as Fancy was satisfied that we were settled in on the porch and her girls were safe she walked out into the yard and collapsed. She was asleep in a minute.

"Told you she'd go outside if we did," I said to Matt.

He nodded. He looked as exhausted as I was. He'd agreed to bring the babies to me for middle of the night feedings so he'd been as sleep-deprived as I was the last few days.

But he at least had the military training that let him drop immediately back asleep, so he was actually in much better shape than I was. Plus, he was not having his nutrients sucked out of his body to support his spawn.

(Don't get mad at me. I loved my girls with my whole heart. But that is what happens.)

We'd just settled into a happy stupor when I saw Spots on the edge of the woods. Fancy saw him, too. Her head lifted and she stared right at him.

"Fancy," I called. "Leave him be. He needs us. If he

jumps that fence, you stay right where you are and do not chase him off, you hear me?"

I know, that was a lot to tell her, but I figured it was worth a try.

When Fancy was a puppy she was too clever for her own good and would eat around whatever you hid a pill in. Cheese, peanut butter, pill pockets. Didn't matter. She'd eat whatever it was and spit out the pill.

Finally, after shoving a pill down her throat for the third time because I had no other option, I looked her in the eyes and told her that she could accept pills with peanut butter or spend the rest of her life having pills shoved down her throat. Her choice.

And from that day forward? She took pills in peanut butter without an issue.

Probably me hallucinating that she understood what I was telling her, but it worked, so I tried it again with Spots.

I handed my baby (Joy) off to Matt and went inside for treats and a doggie ice cream. Before Fancy could scramble to her feet, I put the ice cream in front of her. It was the only thing that might keep her occupied for more than thirty seconds.

While Fancy diligently licked away at her ice cream, I approached the gate in the fence, treats in hand.

"Come here, Spots," I coaxed. "That's a good boy. Look what I've got for you." I opened the side gate and motioned for him to come inside, holding a Pumpkin Puff in my hand.

I glanced back at Fancy. She was still licking away at the ice cream, but watching us. Once she's started in on an ice cream she won't abandon it until it's all gone.

"Come on, Spots. Come on. You've gotta be exhausted, buddy. Come on. Let us take care of you."

He hesitated for another moment and then came forward and took the treat from my hand. He was in rough shape. I could see his ribs and his coat was a mess and that cut on his nose looked even worse than before.

And the amount of dirt and pine needles he was carrying around...

I knelt down and held my hand out and let him sniff it. He did so, but was still tensed to run away.

I offered him another treat and gently scratched behind his ears as he ate it. "That's a good boy, Spots. Good boy."

"Come on." I motioned him through the gate and he stepped through, taking another treat from my hand.

Fancy finished her ice cream and got to her feet. I glared at her. "Fancy...Be nice."

She gave me a look and then ambled over to sniff at Spots. He tensed at first, but didn't move away as she sniffed him over. Slowly, his tail started to wag.

Before I could stop them they were running through the yard, playing.

I watched them intently, waiting for any sign things were going to turn ugly, but they didn't. They played for about two minutes and then both collapsed side by side in the yard.

I smiled and looked at Matt.

He sighed. "I take it we have a new dog."

"Maybe. If his new owner doesn't want him back. But what we definitely need to do is get that guy a good bath and vet visit ASAP. Which means we better tuck the girls away for now so you can take care of that."

"Me? I thought you wanted an outing."

"I did, but no idea how long it'll take to sort all that and well…" I gestured at myself and then the kids. "Unfortunately, not all parenting duties can be done by both parents."

CHAPTER 31

Fancy didn't know what to do with herself when Matt left with Spots. She wanted to watch the girls, but she also didn't want to lose her new best friend. She ended up stationing herself by their cradles but facing the front door of the cabin and didn't move from there until Matt returned with Spots three hours later.

Luckily, since the resort was almost ready to open he'd been able to take Spots to the groomers in the main resort building and call in the vet we'd hired to work the property. (A new vet, I was so excited.)

Spots gave the groomers quite the challenge, because he really was an absolute dirty mess. They had to almost shave him in a few places which meant he came back looking spotted in a whole new way. But the vet declared him surprisingly healthy. His nose had needed some cleaning and two stitches, but that was it.

He looked like a new pup when Matt brought him back home. He seemed to feel like one, too, because he was full of energy. He and Fancy raced out the back the minute Matt walked him through the door and they didn't come back for a full ten minutes, after which they sprawled in the middle of the living room, their paws covered in mud.

I sighed. "Well, I never was one for cleanliness."

"Me neither," Matt said, but we were both staring at those muddy, muddy paws. "Maybe we should think about hiring someone to come and clean once a week now that we have two babies and two dogs."

I wrinkled my nose. "I don't like people in my stuff. I'd have to clean before they came to clean." I turned to look at him. "Did you say two dogs?" I grinned.

He nodded. "If we can keep him. Have you called yet?"

I shook my head. "No. Not yet."

I really didn't want to. Somehow I'd fallen in love with the shaggy little mutt and I didn't want to lose him. I knew it was the right thing to do, so we'd do it. Eventually. Just...maybe in a few more days?

(I know, I know. Somewhere out there his current owner was probably frantic to find him. It wasn't nice to hold onto him for a few days. Which is why we didn't try to.)

"Give me the number. It'll be the last thing I do as a cop." Matt pulled out his phone.

"Okay." I read the number off to him and went to slump down on the couch as he called the shelter down in Denver.

The woman gave him the same runaround she'd given me so he got all official and told her to look him up online and call back through the police switchboard if she didn't trust him.

(I was surprised she didn't pull out the "just because you're a cop doesn't mean you aren't a stalker" card to shut him down, but she didn't.)

She did, however, call back through the main number for the police department. Fortunately, Marlene, the receptionist at the police station, put the call through to Matt's cell instead of saying he didn't work there anymore.

After a little more convincing, he finally had a phone number to call.

I bit my lip as he dialed the number. All I could hear from where I was sitting was his side of the conversation.

He explained that we'd found Spots and where and why we thought he'd run away. And then he nodded and uh-uh'ed in sympathy as the person on the other end of the line talked. "No, yeah, that is rough," he said once before going back to non-committal sounds of agreement.

My fingernails were digging grooves in my palms by then, but Matt has the patience of a saint.

Finally, when it seemed the person on the other end of the line had wound down with whatever they had to say, he said, "We're happy to bring Spots back to you if you want him back. Changing homes is hard on a dog and we want what's best for him."

I sighed. Well, adding Spots to our family had been a nice thought but looked like it wasn't going to happen.

He continued, "But it sounds like you've had a rough time of it lately and if you don't think you're up to taking him back I can promise you we'll give him a great home. He's already bonded with our existing dog and he'll be living in his old home and have a yard and everything. Your call."

I sat up, holding my breath. Was there a chance? Were we going to get to keep Spots?

Matt did some more of that uh-uh nonsense and then he hung up.

"So?" I asked. "You didn't write down an address. Is he…ours?"

He nodded.

"Yes." I pumped my fist in the air. "But, what happened? Why didn't they want him back?"

"It was a young couple who adopted him. But they lost him on a hike near Winter Park. Let him off leash and he kept going. They did try to find him, but no luck."

"They didn't call shelters or anything, though."

He shrugged. "He was microchipped so they assumed they'd get a call when he was found."

"Huh." Me and Fancy, I'd never stop driving around until I found her. I'd camp out in that park and hand out flyers and call everyone and anyone I could think of. But, okay, whatever. Different strokes and all.

"Maggie, don't judge."

I shrugged that off. I always judge. That's like telling water not to be wet. "So that's how they lost him, why don't they want him back?"

"They split up. The woman did want him back, but she's now living in an apartment and the pet deposit, pet rent, etc. would push her over the edge financially. Also, she said he's pretty high energy for an apartment. She made it sound like he might be pretty high energy for a yard."

I looked at the sleeping dog on the floor and raised my eyebrows.

"She said he escaped their yard more than once."

"Oh that I'm not surprised about. He can hop that fence out there no problem. But maybe he kept escaping because he wanted to come home."

"Maybe."

I narrowed my eyes at him. "It doesn't sound like you had to lie to her, though, so why did you?"

"About what?"

"About him living in his old home."

Matt's eyes got a little wide.

"Matt? What aren't you telling me?"

"It was supposed to be a surprise."

I leaned forward. "What was?" I was on the edge of my seat with excitement.

"Maggie…"

"No. No. You said it, you now have to tell me."

He shook his head. "Fine. It's almost ready anyway. We got the house. Not just to rent, to buy. Mason made us a good deal."

I stared at him wide-eyed. "We got the house?" I stood up and did a little jig. "Then why aren't we living there right now?"

He laughed. "Because even when both parties want to you can't just buy a house in a day."

"So we rent it or whatever until the closing."

"Also…"

"What? Just tell me. If we can move out of this cabin and into a real home, Matt, why haven't we?"

He shook his head. "Do you like orange shag carpet and brown wooden kitchen cabinets?"

"No. They're hideous. But, a home. Our home."

"And would you want to renovate those things while we're living there with two newborns?"

"Of course not. I just figured we'd live with it for the time being."

Which, granted, probably meant living with it for the next decade. Something that did not seem all that appealing when I stopped to think about it. But newborns and home reno? Not a good combination.

"Well, lucky for you, and me, for us, your friends and family like you very much. *Our* friends and family like us very much. Jamie is overseeing a whirlwind renovation of the house. Jack and your grandpa have chipped in with free labor. And Greta has used her questionable connections to make things happen I wouldn't have thought possible. Another five days or so and it'll be like a brand new home."

I stared at him. "Really? You mean we get the home and it will be all new and shiny?"

He nodded.

I smiled. But then a thought occurred to me. I opened and closed my mouth. My grandpa had always told me not to look a gift horse in the mouth, so all I said was, "That's great."

"Maggie..."

"It is. It's great. I'm so happy."

"How come you don't sound happy?"

I licked my lips. "I am happy. I am so, so grateful that they're doing this for us."

I pressed my lips together so I wouldn't say anything else.

"But...? Maggie I know you. Just spit it out, whatever it is."

I sighed. "Fine. It's incredibly generous and I am so, so grateful. But...What colors are they using? Because if they went with realtor gray it will make me sad...And are they using carpet? Because Fancy and those modern floors that everyone likes so much do not go well together. I know it's weird, but I like carpet, Matt. And have you seen Jamie and Mason's house? All that wood and stone. I can't live like that."

He laughed, loud and from the belly.

"What? I'm serious."

"I know." He came over and gave me a kiss on the forehead. "Don't you think your family know you well by now? That they know your tastes? And the colors you like? Look at the quilts that Elaine made. Look at the cradles that your grandpa made. Did you like those?"

I nodded. "They were perfect."

"So don't you think that if your best friend, who is the one who told Elaine what colors to use, and your grandpa, who made those cradles, are in charge of this project that they might come pretty close to what you want?"

I chewed on my thumbnail. "Yeah, I guess. You're right. It might not be exactly what I would've chosen, but they know me. I'm sure it'll be amazing." I beamed at him. "And we'll have the perfect home, Matt. That's all ours."

"We will. It's perfect. And, as it turns out, big enough for at least one more kid."

"No. Give me time for some amnesia about pregnancy and childbirth before you even try to go there. Because right now two sounds like a good number."

I settled back into the couch, smiling. We were going to have a house. A renovated house. And we were going to own it. But then something occurred to me and I frowned.

"What now?" Matt asked.

"I was just thinking about my grandpa and how he's going to feel about us moving away. We were next door before and now…"

"Oh, well, that's more news."

"What?"

"Your grandpa is selling his place so he can move in with Lesley."

"When did that happen? Why does no one ever tell me anything?"

Just then Joy started to cry and I went to pick her up and feed her.

Matt nodded towards the babies. "You were pretty busy the last few weeks. We figured you didn't need to know everything."

But I did. I did need to know everything.

I would've argued with him further about that, but between dealing with Joy and then Hope waking up, too, I had to let it drop.

Maybe I did have enough on my plate already. Still. I did not like being left out of the loop.

CHAPTER 32

It took another two weeks for the house to be ready. But the nice part of that was that by the time we finally were able to see the house and move in everyone we knew and loved was also fully vaccinated which meant we could have a real, honest-to-goodness house-warming party.

(Ah, the good old days when vaccines were much more effective…How I miss thee.)

The house was painted a nice deep blue with white trim and had a bright turquoise door for a pop of color. I loved it even more than the first time I'd seen it.

And inside…Jamie led me straight to the nursery.

It was already a little late for it to matter but she'd included a border along the top of the walls that was white with black geometric shapes. Below that the walls were a deep teal that was absolutely gorgeous.

The teal was accented with bright yellow and orange stuffed animals on the shelves and on the pillows on the nursing chairs (one for Matt, one for me). Elaine's quilts matched perfectly and the room looked like it was made to host the cradles my grandpa had made.

It was a peaceful haven built just to my tastes.

And the kitchen…The kitchen was heaven.

My friends and family really did know me. Through some miracle I probably didn't want to look too closely at they'd found me a blue Sub-Zero fridge.

When I saw it I turned to Jamie, wide-eyed. "Jamie…"

"You have been talking about how you want one of those fridges since you were twenty and saw it in a design magazine."

"But, you know why I never bought one. They're pricey."

"Greta said to consider it a baby gift."

Since Greta wasn't there to argue with, I continued my inspection.

The lower cabinets in the rest of the kitchen matched the fridge. The top cabinets were light gray. (Thankfully no white painted cabinets. Those things get *dirty*.) And the countertops were white quartz, not granite. Jamie really did know me well.

But quartz…Once more I looked at Jamie, but she just shook her head. "Mason said to tell you that the upgrade expenses were a great way to reduce the taxable amount of the sale and to stop complaining."

I frowned at her. "Tax write-off or no, the money was still spent. That's like people who don't want to earn too much because they'll have to pay a higher tax rate on the extra income. At the end of the day, it's still more money in their pocket even at the higher rate."

She shrugged and smiled serenely. "Take it up with him. I was just the designer."

"Liar."

"Then take it up with Matt. He's the one who negotiated the house price with Mason that included all of this."

I narrowed my eyes, but only nodded. I knew Matt. He'd accept some help from others, but not too much, so I expected the negotiation with Mason had involved Matt negotiating the price *up* enough to make him feel like it was a fair deal for the house we actually got.

"Well, thank you. For the design help." I gave her a hug.

"Wait until you see the rest of it…"

It was all amazing. There was a home office. With a built-in floor to ceiling bookcase along the longest wall that was already crammed full with all of my books. And all my little tchotchkes. The mementos I'd picked up on travels around the world.

Matt joined us there. "What are all these?" he asked, picking up a vase with a dolphin painted on the side.

"Memories. I bought that one in Greece. And this line drawing of a baby tiger I bought in Prague. And this little carved stone elephant I bought in Spain. Don't you collect things like that?"

He shook his head.

Glancing around the room I laughed. "That's probably a good thing. I don't know where we'd put it all if we were both quasi-hoarders."

He looked a little wide-eyed at the sheer number of books and things on the shelf, so I gave him a kiss on the cheek. "Don't worry. Now that we have the kiddos it'll probably stop."

Jamie laughed. "Maggie, as long as I've known you, you've always had a book in hand. Always. I don't think that's going to stop, even with kids."

"Okay, so maybe not the books. But the things, because, really, when are we ever going to travel again?"

A Puzzling Pooch and Pumpkin Puffs

"Mason and I are already talking about Max's first trip to Paris. You know you can travel with kids."

"Theoretically," I said. "But I have seen those parents at airports with their kids and their carriers and their exhausted, panicked expressions. I'll wait until my kids are like six for that kind of trip, thank you."

"So be it. Well?" She waved her hand through the air. "Are you happy?"

I nodded. "I am. This is amazing." I gave her a quick hug. "It's perfect, Jamie. Thank you."

Mason walked into the room and I turned to him arms spread wide. "Come here. You, too. Thank you."

He shook his head and held his hands out in front of his chest, fending me off. "A thank you is enough. No hugs needed."

"Mason. This may be the only time in our lives I like you this much. Just go with it." I opened my arms again.

"Fine. But make it fast."

(Just for that I hugged him for an extra five seconds and then winked at him when I pulled away.)

I smiled at the room once more. It was amazing. "Okay, I need to go find everyone else involved in this and thank them, too. You guys are the best."

🐾 🐾 🐾

Later that afternoon we all gathered in the backyard for barbecue and burgers. It felt good to be there with that taste of spring in the air and all our friends gathered round. Everyone was laughing and smiling and talking about how excited they were for the new resort.

I stood off to the side, Fancy at my feet, and took it all in.

Greta and Jean-Philippe were sitting at the picnic table whispering quietly together, their hands intertwined. Abe and Evan joined them, all smiles, and I saw Abe reach for the ultrasound picture in his pocket.

I think I'd already seen it myself three times that day. They had baby fever like I have never seen before. It was adorable.

My grandpa and Jack were standing next to the fence having a spirited conversation as they gestured at the boards and around the yard. They were up to something, that's for sure, but I didn't know what.

Sam, red-hair flopping into his eyes, was chasing after Spots, laughing and screaming his head off with glee as Spots barked happily.

Elaine and Dennis stood together in the doorway talking to Mason looking mildly nervous, but definitely comfortable with one another.

Lesley was bustling around with a pitcher of lemonade refilling everyone's glasses while Trish brought out the onion dip, chips, and veggie trays.

Matt was inside checking on the babies who'd gone down for their afternoon nap.

Jamie came over and handed me a bottle of Wooly Booger. "We did pretty good, didn't we? Who would've thought three years ago that we'd be here, now, with all of this."

(Don't worry. Before you freak out about my bad mothering because I was drinking a beer while breastfeeding, I'd done my research. Jamie and I had both banked enough extra milk to let us have one lousy beer at the housewarming without it impacting our kids. Mason and Matt were on baby-feeding duty for the rest of the day and happy to do it.)

I clinked my bottle against hers. "We did do pretty

good, didn't we? Cheers to us. Could you imagine if we hadn't moved here? With the last year?"

She shuddered. "I'd rather not."

We each took a sip of our beer and turned back to watch the small little community we'd built of family, and friends that were like family.

Finally, in that moment I understood why you'd want your family and friends working alongside you to build a business like we were.

Losing so many people so young I'd learned to do it all myself. Better that than to turn around and find that someone you relied on wasn't there anymore. The first time I tried to call my mom after she was gone and remembered she wasn't there…

It had been hard. And I'd had to handle that heartbreak all alone.

And then I'd gone out into the bigger world that pushes us all into these isolated little family units and then makes us so busy we're just struggling to keep our own heads above the water…

It had never occurred to me to look around and offer to help. Or to ask for help.

But there we were, stronger together. I could finally see that. It was hard to accept, and scary to think about relying on others that way.

There was still a small part of me that worried I'd lose one of these people and be all alone again. Or that they'd let me down somehow. But I couldn't let that fear keep them at arms' length anymore

I had to trust. I had to open up. So we could all succeed. Together. So we could *all* have a better life.

Jamie and Mason, Greta and (as weird as it was)

Jean-Philippe, Evan and Abe, me and Matt. Our kids. Our families. All of the other friends we'd made along the way.

It was going to be all of us, working together to pull one another up, to build something from the best of each of us.

(As long as I made sure that Mason and Greta shared out the results equally, but from what I'd seen that wasn't going to be an issue.)

I shook my head.

How had I not wanted everyone I knew and loved involved? How had I thought it would be better to keep it arms' length and distant and professional?

I wiped a tear from my eye as Matt came over and joined us.

"You okay?" he murmured, giving me a quick kiss on the cheek.

I leaned into him. "Couldn't be better."

I knew in the years ahead we'd add more people to our circle, bringing in those who were lost or looking for community, like Elaine. And that there would be new adventures (and mysteries) when the pet resort opened.

But right there in that moment I finally felt complete for the first time since I'd lost my parents. I had everything and everyone I needed.

Life was good. It was really, really good.

CLOSING NOTES

So there we have it. The end of the Maggie May and Miss Fancypants mystery series. As I was finalizing this series I realized that maybe it wasn't so much a cozy mystery series as a small-town family drama with equal amounts of mystery and romance as well as lots of dogs to love.

But, well, a book has to go somewhere on the shelves. And when I started writing this series I had no idea where it was going or how it was going to end and I figured Fancy was such a large part of why I was writing the first story that cozy pet mysteries was as good a fit as any.

Thank you, first and foremost to you, dear reader for sticking through to the end. I selfishly write these books for my own enjoyment but at the end of the day it's readers buying and talking about the books that makes it possible to keep writing.

And so every purchase and every positive review and every reader who comes back for more has a special place in my heart. Especially nine books deep on a wacky little series like this one.

I don't normally write one of these acknowledgement sections because when you self-publish there's not a lot to put into one of these things when it comes to the production side. At least for me.

I don't have an agent or an editor or a cover designer or a book formatter or an advertising team or a foreign rights team to thank. Everything you saw in the last nine books and the related short stories was all me. The good and the bad.

But at the same time, I didn't do this alone.

And while I am fiercely protective of my friends and family and try not to call them out into public because they didn't choose to have me be a writer and they just want to live their lives in peace, I figure here's the place to thank them since if you made it this far (and weren't hate-reading the series for some weird reason that likely requires therapy) then under other circumstances or settings you would be a friend, too.

So let me introduce you to some of the people whose support helped make this happen and maybe give you a little more insight into the series.

First, we have to start with Miss Priss, my real-world version of Fancy.

She's an old lady now. Just celebrated her ninth birthday and I hope will be one of those Newfies who makes it to fifteen. I know that's not likely, but at least she'll always live on in these books.

She's been by my side for every word written and is the reason you have all the little Fancy bits in this series. (Currently she is snoring away right behind me on one of the two dog beds that are in my office. Spoiled? Never.)

She's actually the reason the series exists at all. Because she does in fact like to pee on dead things. Writer-brain took that and thought, "What would happen if she ever peed on a dead body?" and a few years later, off we went.

She's also the one that drags me out for walks and makes sure I eat, mostly because she needs to eat. I hadn't planned on getting a dog at the time she came into my life (I'd been focused on moving to New Zealand), but I wouldn't give up these last nine years for anything.

Next, I should thank all the people and places in Grand County, Colorado in the early 80's. The Baker Valley in these books is made up, as are the characters, but there are definite inspirations in these books from when I lived in the Colorado mountains when I was young.

Grandpa Lou's house in the corner of Creek, for example, is very much inspired by the house we used to live in in Hot Sulphur Springs. And that flat rock on the side of a mountainside that let a little kid watch the train go by while eating sliced peaches covered in sugar absolutely exists.

Although last time I passed through there were too many aspens and too much grass that had grown up on the mountainside to let me reach it. (That's where my dad's ashes are scattered, so it made me sad, but the world changes like that.)

Someone reading these books who was there then will notice some familiar names. Those are my nod to a time and place that I loved. But the characters in these books with those names are not those people.

(I really did write the name MATT on the wall of that house. But that Matt was a cute little toe-headed boy. I have no idea what became of him or my big crush of those years who was a red-headed boy named Sam. Sadly, Sam dumped me in 3rd grade and left me crying to the Grease soundtrack. I'm not sure I ever recovered. Haha.)

After that are my family.

I lost my Grandpa Lee last year. He was part of the inspiration behind Grandpa Lou in the books. I hope I did justice to the core of who he was to me.

The real-life man was a kinder man than Grandpa Lou, and less prone to doling out life advice. But if I were ever in trouble, he would've been the man I wanted in my corner. Just by being himself he taught me some really powerful lessons about life. Although, it might've taken some years for those lessons to sink in...

I want to also thank his widow, Sybil, for reaching out and putting us back in touch after too many years apart. I didn't have the relationship with him that Maggie has with her grandpa, but I am glad that I was able to visit and reconnect before it was too late.

My mom is still very much alive. Every single release she buys five copies of the book in print even though I don't think she has five people to give them to. (Thank you, Mom.)

She's also the only person who gets most of the little "Easter eggs" I've sprinkled throughout the book. (Easter eggs are little inside jokes or references that authors include in stories for those "in the know". Since she was up there in the mountains with me she recognizes the names and places and descriptions. And since she raised me she recognizes the little stories borrowed from my life like the infamous pea incident where I wouldn't eat my peas but she insisted that I do so and we had a three-hour standoff.)

She's also the one who named me Muffie, for better or worse. (That's my real name. And now if you made it to the end of the series, you know why that's my name. Haha. Sigh.)

Thank you, Mom, for reading my books and supporting me with all of this. I appreciate it more than I can say.

I also want to thank my stepdad, Tom, for reading these books. He's far more a reader of Brad Thor-type books, but he's stuck in there until the end. So thank you. Tom, you're a good man and we're lucky to have you in our lives.

Even though he won't read these words, I have to also thank my dad who has been gone for 27 years at this point. No book I write is without his influence. Even all these years later he has a profound impact on who I am and who I became.

He was the best dad I could have hoped for. Not perfect, no one is, but a really, really good dad.

I don't think the rest of my family read these books (and as a writer you can't expect that anyone you know will), but if you're family and you're reading this and I didn't call you out specifically, know that I love you. And I appreciate you making it here to the end with me.

I think I do have some friends who've stuck with this series to this point, too. Thank you to them as well.

You didn't have to, so I hope you made it this far because you enjoyed spending time with a more neurotic version of me. And I appreciate that you're here and also that after reading these books you're still my friend in real life, too.

As a writer I am always both incredibly grateful and somewhat nervous when people I know read what I write. Because the books all come from me, but sometimes they are more than me or they highlight parts of me that I wouldn't highlight in real life.

For those who are readers but don't know me in real life, Maggie's voice is very much my real-life voice. But she's also a version of me that takes all my worst insecurities and instincts and dials them up to ten.

So Maggie is me without normal limits.

I figured if I was going to write a character I might as well give them my flaws because then if people hated the character I could write them off the same way I do in real life when someone doesn't like me. Somehow it's easier to write-off people in real life who don't like me as a person than it is to write-off people online who don't like what I write. It's weird how that works.

Now, I do want to call out one friend in particular, Lindsay.

She is one of my best friends and part of the inspiration behind Jamie in the books.

(Jamie is actually a compilation of my two best friends as well as some additional friends I've had over the years and then some random character traits that none of my close friends have ever had. None have been quite as boy happy as Jamie is.)

Lindsay is a great cook, competent as hell, always put together, and I don't think has ever said a mean word to me even though it's possible she should have at some point. (That's pretty much what it takes to make my close inner friend circle. It's why it's so small. Haha.)

Each time I release a new book she somehow makes

time to read it even though she's juggling two young kids, live-in in-laws, a high-pressure job, and a world that's generally on fire these days.

Sadly we live in different states and I haven't traveled since 2019 so I think at this point it's possible that she's spent more time with Maggie-me than me-me in the last few years, but life does that to you. (Just remember Lindsay, I'm crazy, but not quite as crazy as Maggie.)

Hopefully sometime in the next few years the world will settle down enough for me to visit and we'll get to go out for a dinner involving a tasting-menu and cheese board at some fancy restaurant. I don't care if they're both out of style by then. Cheese is the best. And a surprise meal delivered by a talented chef can't be beat. Especially when paired with good wine.

Okay, then.

I think that's everyone. I'm glad I got to write this series. I'm glad there were readers who read it. This may not be the last of Maggie, Matt, and crew, but it is the end of this series.

I am sorry for anchoring it to the events of the last few years. But I hope I did so with some humor. No matter how dark times get, there's always beauty and humor to be found. Remember that as we go forward.

Anyway. I'm glad you're here. I appreciate your support more than I can express. And may we meet again on the pages of another novel someday. Until then I wish you laughter, health, happiness, and good books to read.

ABOUT THE AUTHOR

When Aleksa Baxter decided to write what she loves it was a no-brainer to write a cozy mystery set in the mountains of Colorado where she grew up and starring a Newfie, Miss Fancypants, that is very much like her own Newfie, in both the good ways and the bad.

🐾 🐾 🐾

You can reach her at <u>aleksabaxterwriter@gmail.com</u> or on her website <u>aleksabaxter.com.</u>

Made in the USA
Las Vegas, NV
20 June 2022

50495913R00108